THE GIFT

THE GIFT

Andrew Puckett

This first world edition published in Great Britain 2000 by
SEVERN HOUSE PUBLISHERS LTD of
9–15 High Street, Sutton, Surrey SM1 1DF.
This first world edition published in the U.S.A. 2000 by
SEVERN HOUSE PUBLISHERS INC of
595 Madison Avenue, New York, N.Y. 10022.

British Library Cataloguing in Publication Data

Puckett,   Andrew
  The gift
  1.   Jones, Tom   (Fictitious character) - Fiction
  2.   Farewell, Jo (Fictitious character) - Fiction
  3.   Fertility clinics - Great Britain - Fiction
  4.   Detective and mystery stories
  I.   Title
  823.9'14 [F]

  ISBN 0-7278-5560-3

All situations in this publication are fictitious and
any resemblance to living persons is purely coincidental.

Typeset by Palimpsest Book Production Ltd.
Polmont, Stirlingshire, Scotland.
Printed and bound in Great Britain by
MPG Books Ltd, Bodmin, Cornwall.

For Laurence James (Laurie) Minall, DFM, 1916–1998.

Acknowledgements

I would like to acknowledge the help I have had in writing this book, as always, from Carol Puckett. Also, sincere thanks are due to Professor William Ledger and Coomber Security Systems Ltd for their expertise and patience.

One

If anyone had told me I'd ever agree to work with Tom Jones again, I'd have laughed at them. If they'd told me how it would end, I'd have wept. Correction – I'd have been at Birmingham International, queuing for the first plane out.

It was exactly five minutes to twelve when the phone in my office rang; I know that because I was staring at the clock at the time, willing it to reach midday.

"Can I speak to Sister Farewell, please?" said a rounded, educated voice.

"Speaking."

"It's Marcus Evans here, Miss Farewell. I don't know whether you remember me?"

The name took about half a second to register, then I laughed. "How could I forget? How are you, Mr Evans?"

"I'm well, thank you. And you?"

"Oh, fine, thanks." It's what people expect you to say, so I said it.

"Good. I was wondering whether we could meet for lunch. On me, of course."

"Are you here? In Latchvale?"

"Yes, I should have mentioned it earlier. Sorry." Ever the gentleman.

"No, don't worry about it, I'd love to. When and where?"

"When and wherever you like. I'm at the main entrance of the hospital at the moment."

"I'll be with you in a few minutes," I said, and put the phone down.

1

Mary, my deputy, was at the desk in the Duty Room.

"I have to go out for a while," I told her. "There aren't any problems are there?"

"No."

"Good. I'll be back as soon as I can."

Inexcusable, but I was feeling very fed up at the time. I quickly changed out of my uniform into the dress I keep in my locker and hurried away.

Marcus Evans – Tom's boss. I hadn't had any contact with Tom for months – he'd be a father by now, I remembered a trifle sourly. It wasn't until I'd nearly reached the main entrance that I wondered what could have brought Marcus up from London. Not me, surely. Something in Birmingham perhaps, although whatever it was must have been rather early in the day, or late, for him to be available for lunch now.

And there he was, his bald dome of a head and black walrus moustache marking him out immediately from the rest of the crowd.

"Hello, Miss Farewell, it's good to see you again." He shook my hand formally. "Good of you to spare me the time at such short notice." He was wearing a dark suit, as he nearly always did.

"Rubbish, I was glad of the excuse to get away."

"Were you?"

"Boring day."

"I find that rather hard to believe in an Intensive Care Unit."

"Oh, I'm just feeling rather jaded at the moment."

"I'm sorry to hear that." Something in the watchfulness of his dark-brown eyes told me he wasn't all that sorry, which should have warned me. "Still, where would you suggest we go for lunch?"

"D'you have a car?"

"I'm afraid not. I came by train."

"And mine's at home. Never mind, we'll go across the park to the Hind's Head, it's only about five minutes."

The Gift

It was early April and the park was at its best: the daffodils were out; leaves were emerging from buds on the trees; and birds were singing in a warm blue sky. We exchanged pleasantries about the season until we were nearly halfway across, then I said abruptly. "How *is* Tom?"

"He's very well. He's a father now, you know. A boy, they've called him Harry."

"I somehow couldn't imagine Tom with a daughter," I observed drily.

Marcus laughed. "No. He wanted a son, and he got one. Funny how things like that seem to go his way." He paused. "You said just now you were jaded. Work?"

"Among other things. The hospital's recently become an NHS Trust, and because of that, I've got a new boss, who's insisted I re-write all our standard operating procedures, not to mention safety precautions."

"Ah." He managed to put a world of understanding into the syllable. "How far are you with it?"

"Oh, it's just about finished now, but it's been an absolute pain. I've become a glorified administrator, which isn't why I took up nursing. No offence intended." I added quickly. Marcus is an administrator, albeit one with a difference.

He smiled. "None taken."

By now, we'd emerged from the other end of the park into the street.

"That, I imagine, is the Hind's Head." He nodded towards the sign.

"Yes." As we started towards it, I said, "Mr Evans, you haven't told me yet what's brought you here."

"I think we know each other well enough for Marcus and Jo now," he said. "Don't you?"

I smiled at him. "Yes. But you still haven't told me . . ."

"Let's wait until we're inside, shall we?"

He bought some drinks and asked what I recommended to eat, and I said cottage pie. Sounds pretty ordinary, I know, but the Hind's home-made version is a million miles

3

from the swamp and sawdust they serve up at the canteen.

We found a table and sat down. I took a mouthful of shandy and lit a cigarette.

"What is it, Marcus? I'm not waiting until we've finished eating."

"We need your help, Jo," he said simply.

"In what way?" I didn't have to ask who we meant.

He took a breath and steepled his fingers. "As you know, part of my job is to screen allegations of crime, serious crime, that concern the Department of Health, and decide which ones bear investigating."

"I do know that," I said gently. "You're procrastinating."

He smiled. "Yes, I am, aren't I? The point is that ReMLA, the Reproductive Medicine Licensing Authority – that's the body that inspects and licences fertility clinics – has come to me with a rather disturbing story."

"About a fertility clinic?"

"Yes. As you know, assisted fertility methods have been in the news a lot lately: there was the woman of fifty-nine who had twins; the black woman who insisted she wanted a white baby because she thought it would have a better chance in life." He sighed. He was still procrastinating.

"So what was the disturbing story?" I asked.

"I can't go into the details now," he said deliberately, "not unless you agree to help us, but a woman who was undergoing fertility treatment apparently overheard the staff saying that the embryos they were implanting in her had not been fertilised by her husband."

"Sperm donation, you mean, that's not so unusual these days."

"Not in this case, no. The clinic had specifically stated that the baby would be her husband's."

"Unethical, no doubt, but does that really count as a serious crime? Besides, DNA testing after the birth would soon prove it one way or the other, and they could sue."

4

"There won't be a birth in this case. The woman died, apparently from an infection, shortly after she'd told her husband what she'd overheard."

"I see," I said slowly. "And you suspect the clinic might have . . . ?"

"I don't know," he said. "ReMLA held an enquiry at the time and found it to be a *bona fide* accident, but that was before the husband came to them with his story."

"Have you met him? The husband."

"Yes."

"And you believe him?"

"I do, yes."

"So what do you think this clinic is up to?"

"I don't know, that's why I want them investigated."

"So how do I come into it?" I asked. "Fertility's not really my area. Can't you send in Tom as an inspector or something?"

"They've just had one inspection," he replied. "Besides, for this sort of investigation, you need the kind of cover that involves you staying overnight. We think a married couple with infertility problems would be the best bet." He hesitated. "We were hoping to persuade you to go with Tom as his wife."

It took a second for it to sink in. "Of all the bloody cheek—" I began, but at that moment, the waitress arrived with the cottage pie.

"This does look good," Marcus said fulsomely as she put it down in front of him.

"Of all the blood—" I began again as soon as she was gone.

"Jo," he interrupted. "We can't really eat this and talk meaningfully at the same time, can we?"

It was all very well for him to switch off, not so easy for me. I picked up a fork, picking with it at the food, and reflected . . .

I was pretty fed up. There had been problems in my life other than work, namely, the death of my father, and the break-up of my relationship with Colin Anslow.

The truth was, I suppose, that I'd used Colin as a substitute for Tom, and yet I had become fond of him, grown accustomed to him as a rock to lean on.

I don't know what it was that attracted me to Tom, let's face it, he's nothing special. Somewhere in his thirties (late, probably), average height (a shade under, if anything), brown hair and eyes and a rather hard, ferrety face. Not as good-looking as Colin, and nothing like so considerate.

And I'm not generally regarded as such a bad catch myself. I'm twenty-six, I have long chestnut hair, hazel eyes, small features (Colin said I had the face of a depraved elf), and not a bad figure.

But I knew Tom would never leave his wife for me, especially not now that he had a son. And I'm not sure I'd have wanted that anyway.

But to be asked to pose as his wife, his infertile wife at that – talk about pouring vitriol into a wound.

I couldn't eat any more so I pushed my plate away, lit another cigarette and to hell with bad manners; besides, Marcus's little bombshell hadn't been exactly tactful.

"I take it you don't want a pudding," he said with a faint smile after he'd finished.

"No." I blew smoke. "You realise your proposition wasn't only offensive, it was hurtful."

"Yes, I do realise that." He looked me in the eyes and I could see that he did. "But it's important."

"Why me?"

He leaned forward. "Because you'd be the best. Because you've worked with Tom before, worked well, whatever your relationship was."

"That was self-preservation."

"Even so . . ."

"Even if I were willing. I'd never get the time off. We're talking at least a month, aren't we? Probably nearer two."

"That's not a problem. It would be a sabbatical for as long as it took."

I believed him. I'd seen for myself that underneath the politeness and diffidence, he had real clout.

Then, I had a revelation.

"How much would I be paid, Marcus?" I asked slowly. "On top of my normal salary."

"I thought around four or five thousand, double your normal salary, let's say—"

"I want at least ten thousand."

The cogs turned in his brain, then he said quietly, "I hadn't envisaged that much. But I will look into it, see how much we can afford." He hadn't expected nice little Nurse Farewell to be so mercenary.

"In that case," I said, "I'll consider it." My heart beat faster as I said this; I think we both knew what consider meant.

"Good," Marcus said softly. Then, "I think the next step is for you to come down to London so that we can discuss it in more detail."

"When?"

"Today's Friday. Could you come on Monday?"

"Tuesday's probably best for me."

"We'll say Tuesday, then." He took an envelope from his pocket and handed it to me. "Directions on how to find us, and a rail warrant."

"You were certainly sure of me."

"No, not at all," he said. "Just hopeful. Another drink?"

"No thanks, I'd better be getting back." I wanted to go, wanted to think about it away from him.

We didn't say much as we walked back through the park, but it wasn't an uncomfortable or unfriendly silence, just charged somehow. The blue of the sky was more electric, the daffodils more fulgent, the birdsong more vibrant. All in the mind, doubtless.

We said goodbye at the main entrance and I walked away without looking back, allowing the implications of what I'd agreed to consider to float to the surface.

My father had been a lovely man, a cabinet-maker, a true

craftsman. And because he'd been so good at his craft, he'd been reasonably well paid, by his standards anyway. But both he and my mother had been children where money was concerned. After we'd buried him, my mother and I discovered that although he'd left her adequately provided for, there was still a mortgage outstanding on the house. There was an insurance policy and Dad had obviously assumed this would pay off the outstanding amount after his death, but the small print had dictated otherwise.

Neither my mother nor I wanted us to live together – not because we didn't have a good relationship, we did and we wanted to keep it that way. And not surprisingly, for the sake of continuity, she wanted to stay in her own house. I'd made arrangements for a bank loan to cover the mortgage, but the interest was going to take a large bite out of my already stretched salary. Strange how the low interest rates we'd heard so much about weren't reflected in bank loans! And my Mini was beginning to make retirement noises. It had never really recovered from its violent embrace with Tom's car. Rather like me and Tom, really . . .

The amount owing on the house? You've guessed it – ten thousand pounds.

Two

There's always something exciting about arriving in a big city, especially by train, and especially when it's London. Perhaps it's the way the buildings become larger, more concentrated, more dominating, until you feel as though the train is burrowing through them, then the final plunge into darkness before arrival at the terminus, with its echoing whistles and taxi horns – so much more civilised than an airport.

Following Marcus's directions, I took the tube to Westminster, then walked along Whitehall until I found the right building, where I was shown up to his office.

Marcus and the two others with him stood up as I came in. One was Tom, the other, a tall, spare man in a grey suit.

"Good morning, Jo." Marcus greeted me. "Good journey?"

"Fine, thank you."

"Jo, may I introduce Professor Fulbourn, who's head of the Department of Reproductive Medicine at St Michael's, and also the national collator of statistics concerning fertility clinics. Professor, this is Sister Jo Farewell of St Chad's in Latchvale."

"How d'you do, Sister?" he said as he stepped forward to take my hand. His deep, incisive voice had a touch of the north about it and he had a long, lined face and aquiline nose with a somehow military moustache beneath it. He looked to be in his sixties.

Marcus said, "Tom, you already know, of course."

"Hello, Jo," Tom said softly.

"'Lo, Tom."

"Have a seat, Jo," Marcus said, indicating one, and we all sat. "We're waiting for Dr Ashby, the microbiologist attached to ReMLA. We'll have some coffee when he arrives, unless you particularly want one now, of course?"

"No thanks," I said, although I could have done with one.

"You had no difficulty in finding us, then?"

"None. Your directions were very clear."

There was a short silence. To break it. I said, "I understand you're to be congratulated, Tom."

"Thank you."

"How are you finding parenthood?"

"I like it."

"Is your wife well?"

"Thank you, yes."

I don't know how long I'd have kept this up if there hadn't been a knock on the door. Marcus's secretary put her head round it.

"It's Dr Ashby, Mr Evans."

"Good. Come in, Miles."

"Shall I bring the coffee now, Mr Evans?"

"Please."

As soon as she'd gone, Marcus introduced us to Ashby, a plumpish man of medium height, with thinning, sandy hair, gold-rimmed glasses and an engaging smile. The coffee arrived. Marcus asked Tom to be mother (Tom's lip curled as he caught me repressing a smile), then opened the proceedings.

"I've called this meeting so that we can pool our knowledge concerning the death of Mrs Tracy Murrell at Catcott Manor Fertility Clinic, and then decide on what action, if any, should be taken. Miles, since you conducted the enquiry, perhaps you'd like to start by outlining for us the facts of the Murrell case?"

"Certainly." Ashby took a sheaf of papers from his briefcase, cleared his throat and began speaking in his pleasant, light voice.

The Gift

"Catcott Manor is a small, private fertility clinic on the edge of Salisbury Plain in Wiltshire. It's been open for about five years and is owned by a company called Fertility Enterprises, which, so far as I can ascertain, doesn't own any other clinics. The Medical Director is Dr Davina Kent, there are also a Scientific Director, three qualified nurses and a lab worker. They used to do mainly conventional IVF work, but they've always been interested in male infertility, and since acquiring microinjection equipment two years ago have tended to specialise in male fertility problems. The building is leased from National Heritage and the lease has only another six months to run. I understand National Heritage doesn't intend renewing it." He paused and looked round briefly before continuing.

"Mr and Mrs Trevor Murrell were accepted by the clinic two months ago and treatment started at once. Mr Murrell suffers from oligozoospermia, which affects the quality of his sperm. Mrs Murrell took a course of fertility drugs and on" – he consulted his notes – "March the fifth, eggs were collected from her ovaries by laparoscopy, for which she was given a general anaesthetic . . . Professor, you wanted to say something?"

"I'm sorry to interrupt, but did you say her eggs were collected by laparoscopy?"

"Yes, I did."

"Interesting. Ultrasound is usually used these days." He paused. "You didn't mention an anaesthetist among the staff. They'd need one for laparoscopy, you know."

"Indeed. They use a retired consultant who lives nearby, a venerable old chap called Longstreet. This may have some significance, as you will see."

He waited to see whether the Professor was going to say any more, then continued, "From the clinic's point of view, everything proceeded normally. The eggs were passed to the laboratory, where they were fertilised with sperm from Mr Murrell using microinjection. They were then incubated for

11

three days and monitored as they developed into embryos while Mrs Murrell remained at the clinic with her husband to await the eggs replacement in her womb.

"However, before this could happen, she developed a fever and was put on a course of antibiotics. This, unfortunately, was to no avail and she died the same day of an overwhelming group A streptococcal infection."

The short silence was broken by the Professor. "I'm rather surprised antibiotic therapy didn't work."

"It was a highly toxogenic organism – the so-called flesh-eating strain. The antibiotics simply didn't have time to work."

"Was there a post mortem?" This, from Tom.

"Yes, but nothing untoward was discovered."

"You mentioned an enquiry?" said the Professor.

"Yes, we carried it out that week. The clinic's aseptic and other procedures were all satisfactory, none of the staff were carriers and no source of the organism was found. We concluded that Mrs Murrell herself was the carrier."

"Didn't Mr Murrell have anything to say at this time?" Tom again.

"No, he was still in a state of shock. It wasn't until after we'd completed our enquiry and put her death down to misadventure that Mr Murrell came to us with his curious story."

"How long afterwards?" the Professor asked.

"Let me see . . ." Again, Ashby consulted his notes. "March the nineteenth, to be exact. Just under two weeks."

"And what was this curious story, exactly?"

"In essence, that despite the general anaesthetic, Mrs Murrell was conscious during the laparoscopy and overheard one of the staff saying that Mr Murrell would not be the father of the baby."

"I suppose it's possible she was conscious," the Professor mused, "if the anaesthetist had forgotten the pre-med, or given the wrong dose of supplementary anaesthetic." He looked up at Ashby. "You don't think it was vindictiveness, on Murrell's part? Once the death of his wife had sunk in."

The Gift

Ashby shrugged his shoulders. "It could have been, of course." He glanced at Marcus. "It's just that we don't think it was."

"Do you know Mrs Murrell's exact words?" asked the Professor. "We do need that, really."

"You'll appreciate that's not very easy. Mr Murrell isn't the brightest of men, and in the circumstances, his memory wasn't of the best. However . . ." he turned to Marcus again.

"After Dr Ashby had told me about the case, I questioned Mr Murrell myself," Marcus said, "and took the precaution of taping the interview." He picked up a cassette, pushed it into the player on his desk and pressed a button. After a preliminary crackle, his voice came out of the speaker.

"So can you tell me, please, Mr Murrell, what it was that your wife told you?"

"'S difficult, like I told the other guy." Mr Murrell was from the East End of London.

"Just do the best you can."

There was a sigh, then Murrell said, "She was woozy like, after the op. An' they give 'er seddytives to keep 'er quiet."

"Yes?"

"Well. I could'n' get no sense from 'er at first, then the nex' day she says, 'Trev, I'm scared, I don' like it 'ere.' Why not? I says. Seems all right to me. Then she says, 'Trev. I was awake, y' know, in the op.' What? I says. You mean when they cut you open . . . ? No, I didn' feel nuffink,' she says, 'but I 'eard.' 'Eard what? I says. Then she says . . .'" Murrell, whose voice had become unsteady, gulped and swallowed.

"Just take your time," Marcus said.

"She says, 'They was saying the baby wouldn' be yours, Trev, I 'eard 'em.' I says somfink like, 'oo the fuck's is it then? Scuse me, Mr Evans."

"That's all right," Marcus said gently.

We sat in silence as Murrell sniffed. Then, he said, "She didn' say no more after that. The nurse had come in an' gives 'er a jab."

13

"So the nurse was in the room while she was telling you this?" Marcus interrupted quickly.

"Can't remember. She coulda bin, I s'pose."

"Then what happened?"

"She slept, an' when she woke up, she was 'ot like, all over. I tol' the quacks, but they couldn' . . ."

His voice disintegrated and Marcus shut the machine off. After a short silence.

Ashby said, "That's pretty well exactly what he told me."

Marcus looked at Professor Fulbourn. "Not the voice of vindictiveness. I'd have thought."

"No." Prof cleared his throat. "It's still a great shame we don't have Mrs Murrell's exact words, though. As Mr Murrell so trenchantly observed himself, if it wasn't his baby, whose was it?"

Ashby said, "There is one possibility. A man will pay a great deal of money to have a biological child of his own. Mr Murrell paid nearly four thousand pounds, although he's far from wealthy. Suppose the clinic took the money, then simply used donor sperm instead."

"That thought had already occurred to me, as you know," said Marcus, re-asserting his control over the meeting. "But before we go into that, are we all agreed that Mr Murrell's story is, to say the least, a cause for concern?"

"Naturally," said Ashby.

"Yes," said Tom. "Definitely."

I nodded my agreement.

The Professor sighed. "Cause for concern, certainly, I'd have to agree with that. But what can we do about it?"

"That's what we're here to decide," said Marcus. "I think it might be useful at this stage, Professor, if you, as the expert among us, could give us the background to what we've heard, and perhaps explain some of the terms." He looked down at his notepad. "Er . . . oligozoospermia, for instance. Laparoscopy, ultrasound. And microinjection of sperm."

Prof smiled. "That's rather like a person with no basic

physics asking for an explanation of the quantum theory. However" – he looked round – "those of you who already have some knowledge will have to bear with me."

Assuming I was included in that category, I nodded, along with Ashby.

"Forewarned by Evans," continued Prof, "I took the precaution of bringing along a visual aid." He opened his briefcase, took out and hung up the usual flattering portrayal of female internal plumbing. It always reminds me of a wildebeest's skull: the tubes and ovaries forming the horns; the triangular womb, the head: and the cervix and vagina, the snout.

"Pregnancy," said Prof, "is a miracle which occurs when a sperm deposited here, in the vagina, manages the epic journey up through the cervix and womb to the Fallopian tubes, here, where it fuses with an egg which has been released by an ovary. The fertilised egg is then carried back down to the womb, here, where it embeds and becomes an embryo. Clear so far?"

Nods from Tom and Marcus. I glanced at Tom, wondering if he was thinking of his own son. Jealousy twisted at me for an instant and I thought: Must stop this . . .

"One of the most common causes of infertility is blocked Fallopian tubes. Sometimes, they can be unblocked, but all too often, sadly, they can't. In these cases, *in vitro* fertilisation, IVF, is usually the couple's only remaining hope.

"IVF means exactly what it says: fertilisation of an egg by a sperm outside the body, literally, in glass. Although I suppose in plastic might be more accurate these days." He sighed. "I digress. The woman is given a course of fertility drugs so that she produces up to a dozen eggs, and when these have developed, they are collected from the ovaries either by laparoscopy, or ultrasound.

"I'll try and explain both these terms. A laparoscope is a surgical probe with a tiny camera on the end. A small abdominal incision is made, the laparoscope inserted and the eggs collected from the ovaries by remote control using a TV screen. Naturally, this is performed under general anaesthetic. Clear?"

More nods.

"Ultrasound is also what it says. Sound waves are directed through the body like radar, and the returning echoes are used to build up a picture, also on a TV screen. Mr Jones," – he turned to Tom – "I couldn't help overhearing that you'd recently become a father – did your wife have a scan?"

"She did, yes," said Tom. "It was incredible. You could actually see the baby's features on the screen."

Prof nodded and smiled. "Incredible, yes, I suppose it is rather. Anyway, you use this same technique for collecting eggs. A fine needle is passed either through the abdomen or the vaginal wall to the ovaries and, guided by the ultrasound, picks up the eggs. It's quicker than laparoscopy and, since it requires only local anaesthesia, safer."

"So why did they use laparoscopy at Catcott Manor?" I asked.

"A good question. Any ideas. Dr Ashby?"

"I did ask Dr Kent, the director, about this, since they do have state-of-the-art ultrasound equipment and usually use it. She told me that she sometimes uses laparoscopy when the eggs are in a difficult position on the ovaries and she wants to collect them all."

"Is it important?" asked Marcus. "I mean, is there any reason they *shouldn't* have used laparoscopy?"

"Not really, no," replied Prof, "although I avoid using it myself these days, because it involves the use of a general anaesthetic."

I said. "Well, it's certainly something I'd like to know about. I mean, it does rather affect—"

"Indeed," said Marcus, overriding me, "but we'll consider it later, if you don't mind. Professor, you were telling us about IVF."

"Yes. The eggs have now been collected, by whatever method. They're taken to the laboratory, examined, then sperm from the husband is added – in a Petri dish rather than a test tube. Although I suppose Petri Dish Baby doesn't have quite the same ring about it." he added reflectively. "The eggs are then incubated for two or three days and periodically examined to check their development. I usually replace them in the woman's womb when they are at the four-cell stage."

"How is that done?" asked Marcus.

"The embryos are taken up into a fine tube, which is then passed up through the woman's cervical canal into her womb, where they are gently expelled."

"You make it sound simple."

"It is, compared with egg collection."

"What's the success rate?"

"If you replace four embryos, about thirty-five per cent." He smiled. "There's also a chance of multiple births, which is why I never replace more than four."

"How soon d'you know whether you've been successful?"

"About two weeks, perhaps a shade under. By blood tests."

Marcus nodded, made a few notes, then said, "Which brings us to microinjection of sperm."

"Er – any more coffee in that pot, Mr Evans? This talking has made me rather dry."

"Yes, Anyone else?"

We all gratefully accepted refills.

Prof meanwhile had gathered his thoughts.

"I said earlier that blocked Fallopian tubes was one of the most common causes of infertility, but it's far from being the only one. Poor sperm quality is probably the next most common, either because there aren't enough of them, which we call oligozoospermia, or because they can't swim fast enough, which we call asthenozoospermia." He gave one of his wry smiles. "It seems that Western man isn't the man he once was. For some reason, as yet unknown, our sperm quality has been steadily declining, at least for the last fifty years or so, since records have been kept. Perhaps we're doomed to extinction, which is maybe no more than we deserve . . . However, IVF can help in these situations, because the spermatozoa are excused their arduous journey. They're delivered direct to the doorstep, so to speak.

"There are variations on this theme, for instance – Gamete Intra Fallopian Transfer – GIFT – a rather apt and lovely acronym. Sperm and eggs are delivered together to the tubes before fertilisation has taken place. Sometimes this works where IVF has failed, although it's not clear why. Sometimes, even when sperm is placed directly on the egg, the spermatozoa are simply too weak to penetrate it.

"Until very recently, Artificial Insemination by Donor, AID, was the only hope for these couples, but then microinjection was developed. In this technique, the egg is held on a suction tube under a microscope while a spermatozoa is injected directly into it using a very thin glass needle. It's tricky, to say the least, but it can, and does sometimes work." He paused. "I think I'll it leave it there, before you start dropping off to sleep."

"That's not very likely, Professor," Marcus said with a smile. "What's the success rate of microinjection?"

"Very difficult to say. The technique's so new, the few figures we have can't really be relied upon."

"Is Catcott Manor successful?"

"They have some success, certainly. I can't remember the exact figures."

"I see. Thank you, Professor, you've certainly made things much clearer for us." He looked round at us all. "The thing is, what are we going to do about it? Miles, what do you think? You have the advantage of us, you've been there, we haven't."

Ashby took a deep breath and released it. "I think it should be investigated. The thing that bothers me most of all – apart from the Murrell case, obviously – is their, in my view, unnecessarily high level of security."

Tom looked up. "What kind of security?"

"A very sophisticated alarm system, including close-circuit cameras and invisible light beams. They also employ two full-time security guards, one of whom lives on the premises and is positively Neanderthal."

"Have you ever asked them the reason?" said Marcus.

"Yes, I have. Dr Kent justifies it partly on the grounds of threats she says she's received from extremist pro-life groups—"

"But that's ridiculous," said Tom, "Surely, she's bringing about life, not destroying it."

"Embryos are sometimes discarded. Don't you remember all the fuss about embryo research? And many people find the methods by which the embryos have been brought into existence abhorrent."

"You said partly on those grounds." said Marcus.

"Indeed. Her other justification is the expensive equipment she has on the premises."

Marcus nodded. "But you nevertheless regard the level of security as unnecessary?"

"I do." He hesitated, then went on, "And the whole place has an oppressive atmosphere, as though it's hiding something . . . I know that sounds fanciful. but I do feel strongly it should be investigated."

"Unnecessary security, oppressive atmosphere," rumbled the Professor. "Hardly relevant if you've only noticed them now."

"I had noticed them earlier." Ashby said defensively. "but their relevance didn't strike me until the Murrell case."

"Professor," said Marcus, "you can see that the rest of us here feel that there's a – a case to be answered. Don't you feel the same way?"

Prof looked up. "Rather depends on what you propose doing about it."

"I propose sending Mr Jones and Miss Farewell into Catcott Manor pasing as a couple with fertility problems."

Prof paused for a moment, his eyes on his hands. Then, he said, "Don't know why you're asking me, since you're obviously going to go ahead whatever I say."

"Because we need your help, Professor. Your professional help."

Again, the wry smile. "Oh, I see. What kind of help?"

"Miss Farewell and Mr Jones will need a cover story. A verifiable medical history and referral from a bona fide clinic such as yours."

"I see," he said again. "I can foresee one problem straight away. Supposing I were to do as you ask, but that Miss Farewell and Mr Jones were to find nothing, as is quite possible. That could place me in an awkward position, having falsified medical evidence."

"No." Marcus shook his head vigorously. "My department has the authority to ask you to do this; it also has complete responsibility for its actions. In other words. I carry the can."

Prof paused, his eyes flicking round us. "I'm uneasy about what I've heard, naturally. But I'm not convinced that such a cloak and dagger approach is necessary. You'll have to let me think about it."

Marcus swallowed. "I was hoping we'd come to some form of agreement today. Miss Farewell has to go back, and—"

"Won't take me all day." He glanced up at the clock. "It's just gone twelve. I'll let you know by two."

20

Three

The room seemed to sigh as the Professor and Dr Ashby left. Marcus came back in and shut the door.

"So now we wait."

"It stinks and Fulbourn knows it," Tom said. "I think he'll agree."

"Even though it means falsifying medical documents? Lying, in effect."

"Yes, when he thinks about it. But if he won't help, can't you find someone else?"

"I could, but I don't want to. A referral from him will carry the most weight. Look, why don't you two go and have some lunch?"

"Aren't you coming?" said Tom.

"I'm going to wait in case he rings. I'll have a sandwich or something."

"OK. I'll go and get my coat."

"By the way, Jo," Marcus said as the door closed behind Tom, "finance say they're prepared to pay you seven and a half thousand."

"In view of what happened to Mrs Murrell, I'm not sure that's enough."

"I don't think you'll get any more," he said. "It is tax free, remember, and on top of your usual salary."

"I think I'll wait and see what Professor Fulbourn has to say."

"I'll need an answer today, Jo. I'm deadly serious about this, so please don't mess me about." The door opened again and

Tom came back in. "And as for Mrs Murrell, don't worry, it won't happen to you. Tom here'll be with you, and I'll not be far away. Now, off to lunch with you, I want to think."

"Yessir." Tom sketched a salute.

It wasn't until we were on the pavement that Tom said. "Are you really worried about it being dangerous, because I—"

"That's part of it, but only part. I want to hear what the Professor says before I make up my mind."

"Is it because . . . ?"

"I'd like to leave it for now, OK?"

He shrugged and started walking. "OK."

"Where are you taking me? Canteen a bit iffy?"

He laughed. "In Whitehall? Hardly. No, We'll go to a pub I know. Thought it might be an idea to get out for a bit."

His voice was just the same, south London with the edges rubbed off. We walked in silence for a spell. I don't know why I was feeling so prickly. Yes I do.

I couldn't remember ever having walked down Whitehall before, although I suppose I must have done on a school trip. Budding leaves glowed in the strong spring sunlight, which also lit the pale stone of the massive government buildings behind the trees. They certainly looked the part, more than the part, in fact . . . then I remembered that they'd been built in the days when the country was rich and powerful. These were buildings from which nearly a quarter of the globe had been ruled.

"Downing Street," said Tom, pointing to the policeman guarding the barricades across it. "Remember when you could walk up to Number Ten?"

I shook my head. "Before my time."

"I can. And I don't much like the fact that you can't now."

"Progress," I said.

He smiled but didn't say anything more, yet what he had said gave me a sudden insight into why he did the job he did.

He turned down a side street and a couple of minutes later,

we reached the pub. It was called the Harrow and bore a picture of said agricultural implement on its sign, although I suspected that hereabouts, the clientele would identify more closely with the school. Inside, it was long and narrow with a brass rail along the bar. Bare floor, comfortable wooden furniture and not a horse brass in sight. Tom asked me what I wanted to drink.

"Half a shandy, please."

"Have half a bitter, it's too good here to spoil with lemonade."

I shrugged. "OK."

"What about something to eat?"

"What are you having?"

"Ploughman's lunch." Seeing my expression, he said. "It's not like the usual pub ploughman's."

He ordered and, of course, he was dead right. The beer was beautiful and the ploughman's a huge wedge of mature cheddar that tingled pleasantly on the tongue and a hunk – the only possible word – of wholemeal bread that was crusty without being twee.

"I think it's the only place left in the whole country that still does a real ploughman's," he said.

"Get a lot of farm workers here, do you?"

"Not so many, no." He took another bite of bread.

I did the same and looked round. I'd been right about the clientele: pin-stripes and softly murmured accents. An awful lot of them seemed to be eating the same as us, though.

"Seems funny to think of you being a father," I said a few moments later. "Were you at the birth?"

"I was." He smiled. "I didn't want to be at first, but Holly insisted and I'm glad I was now. It was" – his eyes flicked away, then back again – "quite something."

"Does he spoil your beauty sleep much?"

"Not so much now, although I sometimes sneak off to the spare room anyway."

"Typical."

"Well, I've got to go to work in the mornings." He bit off some cheese. "She hasn't."

"So nursing a baby isn't work?"

"Not in quite the same way, no. Besides, what's the point of having two of us tired out?"

"Moral support?"

He ate some more bread and cheese, washing it down with beer.

"I was a bit surprised that you were interested in this job at all, Jo. Thought you'd settled down with that nice Inspector Ansley."

"Anslow. No, it didn't work out and we split up."

"Why was that?"

"If it's any of your business, the demands of our respective jobs. They simply weren't compatible."

"Bullshit," he said softly. "*You* weren't compatible." He and Colin hadn't liked each other.

I shrugged. "If you say so. You always did know my business better than me."

"And that's why you've agreed to consider this job?"

"Yes. D'you really think it's going to go ahead, Tom?" I asked to change the subject.

"I'm sure of it, with or without the good Professor's help. It stinks and this is the only way to find out what's going on."

"Couldn't ReMLA have investigated it themselves? Or handed it over to the police? I'd have thought suspected murder was their job."

"There's no way murder can ever be proved now. And neither of them could investigate without alerting the clinic to the fact. No, ReMLA did the most sensible thing when they came to us." He drank some more beer. "Are you really worried about what happened to Mrs Murrell?"

"Of course I am, a bit."

"So why do I have the feeling you're going to accept?"

"Because I probably will, although I do want to hear what the Professor's got to say. What does Holly think about it?"

"She's not happy, naturally, but she accepts that this sort of thing is part of my job." He regarded me pensively. "Which brings me to another matter."

"Well?"

He lowered his voice. "Holly's pretty tolerant, but I think she guessed there was something between us last year. We really do have to play it straight this time." He gave a deprecatory smile. "Platonic and all that."

"You arrogant bastard!" I rose to my feet without thinking. "Is that why you thought I was going to accept the job?" The pin-striped muttering faded and eyes, although not faces, flickered our way. "Well, you can stick it!" I grabbed coat and bag and marched out. I'd reached Whitehall before he caught up with me.

"Jo, I didn't mean it like that . . ."

"Oh? How did you mean it, then?" I kept walking.

"I just felt that it was something that we ought not to have any misapprehensions about, since—"

"You thought I wouldn't be able to resist your wonderful body."

"No—"

"Well, you can go and tell Marcus why I've gone home."

"Jo, please, he'll fillet me."

"Good."

"We'll never find anyone quite as suitable as—"

"Good.

"But Jo—"

"Leave me *alone*."

I sensed him standing, irresolute. I kept walking. He caught me up at Downing Street.

"Jo, you did misunderstand me."

"I don't think so."

"You see," he swallowed, trying to keep pace with me, "what I was trying to say was that I – I care for you and would find it very difficult to – to resist you. That's what I meant. And I can't afford that now."

"Bullshit." But still, it was quite a slice of humble pie.

"Jo, why did you want the job?"

I stopped dead and looked at him. "Money."

"Money? Marcus did say . . . Are you short of money?"

"Why the hell d'you think I want some so badly?"

"I dunno. Why?"

I told him. His face fell.

"I'm sorry, Jo. If I were to tell Marcus—"

"Was that an apology I just heard, or merely an expression of sympathy?"

"Both. If I told Marcus, maybe he—"

"I'll think about it after the Professor's had his say."

"Let me speak to him, please."

"No. No hard luck stories. I don't want to be in his debt."

Marcus was grinning broadly when we got back. "He's agreed to help," he said. "He wants us to go round and see him at St Michael's at two."

Four

S t Michael's Hospital had been built in the sixties and belonged to the lavatorial-tile school of architecture, although I believe it has a very good reputation. Professor Fulbourn lived on the fourth floor. His secretary showed us to his office along a fluorescent-lit corridor whose walls were covered in photographs of babies. I guessed (correctly) that these were the clinic's successes.

Prof stood up as we were shown in.

"Do take a seat. Tea or coffee? No? Good." He nodded to his secretary who silently withdrew.

"As I told Mr Evans over the phone, I've decided to help you, if I can." He resumed his seat behind his desk.

"We're very grateful, Professor," Marcus said. "Also for your seeing us so quickly."

Prof made a think-nothing-of-it sort of gesture, then continued, "The situation as I see it is that you want me to refer Miss Farewell and Mr Jones to the Catcott Fertility Clinic, so let's firstly consider what your medical histories should be. Are you going as a married couple?"

"We thought so, yes," Marcus answered for us. "Not that it really matters, we just wondered whether it might make acceptance that bit more likely."

"Shouldn't make any difference. Where are you going to be living?"

"If you mean the fictional Joneses, that hasn't finally been decided yet," Marcus said.

"So long as it's not too far from here, since you're supposed

27

to have been treated at this clinic." He turned his attention to Tom and myself. "You would've had to have been trying to conceive for at least two years before I'd have treated you, and we would have tried up to three cycles of IVF before advising you to look elsewhere. So what condition can we give you that will stimulate their interest?" A pause, while he considered us. "I think you, Mr Jones, should have oligozoospermia, which is what Mr Murrell has, but asthenazoospermia as well. This means you have both a low sperm count, and also that less than half the sperm you do have display any forward motility. This is the sort of case that Catcott Fertility Clinic seems to find most attractive now."

Tom gave a forced smile. "I imagine, assuming they accept us, that they'll want to check this for themselves?"

"I'm certain they will, yes. So, how can we mimic this condition?"

"Drugs?"

"Certainly possible. There's a drug we could use called Salazopyrin" – I gave a slight jump – "you recognise it. Sister?"

"Isn't it used to treat Crohn's disease?"

"Correct. D'you remember the side effects?"

"Er . . . nausea and vomiting, I think. Quite severe."

"Yes. Also headaches, skin rashes and epigastric discomfort. You can stop worrying Mr Jones, you'd have to take it for at least two months before it depressed your sperm level sufficiently, and I imagine you're in a bigger hurry than that."

"Er, yes, we are," Tom replied quickly.

"We need to be in there as soon as possible, Professor," said Marcus. "Before they decide to stop doing whatever it is they're doing. Especially in view of the fact that their lease is due to expire before long."

"So we'll have to prepare a specimen for you to take along."

"You can do that?" Tom asked, with some relief.

"I should think so. D'you know how sperm samples are produced for these investigations?"

28

"Er, masturbation. I believe."

"Which, fortunately for you, is something normally done in private. You'll be shown into a cubicle. Stay in there for a realistic amount of time, say, ten or fifteen minutes, then transfer the sample you'll have kept warm in your pocket to the container they'll have given you."

"Won't they be able to tell it isn't from me?"

"It's highly unlikely they'll even try. However, what's your blood group?"

"O positive."

"Good. I'll try and make the specimen the same group. Now, Miss Farewell," he turned to me, "do we need to simulate a condition for you as well, I wonder?"

"I can't honestly see that you do."

"Perhaps not. It would have to be blocked tubes, or possibly antibodies to your husband's sperm, but we don't want to give them any excuse for doing a laparoscopy on you, do we?"

"We do not," I said firmly.

"Very well. I think that your husband's condition will be sufficient explanation for IVF not working." He made notes on his pad. "So, we'll say that you received three cycles of IVF with no result."

I said, "Wouldn't you have tried something else?"

"Possibly GIFT, although I doubt that would have worked any better in your case. And you'd have been offered Artificial Insemination by Donor of course."

"But you, Tom, feeling this slighted your manhood, refused," said Marcus.

"Let's say you were on the point of accepting when you heard about microinjection," said Professor Fulbourn.

"But wouldn't you have told us about microinjection yourself?" I asked.

"I might well have, since we're in the process of evaluating it here. Let's say that I have told you about it, but you decided you didn't want to wait until we started it here."

"Fine," said Tom.

I said, "Yes, fine. But now can we have the bad news about what I'll have to suffer for the cause? Assuming I agree to go through with this, that is." I was becoming a little irritated at the way they were taking my participation for granted.

Professor Fulbourn raised his eyebrows at me. "I was under the impression that you'd already agreed, Sister."

"That rather depends on what you have to say, Professor."

"I see." He glanced at Marcus. "That puts me in rather an invidious position."

"Why not just tell the truth," I suggested.

"Very well." His eyes met mine for a moment. "I can't honestly tell you exactly how unpleasant or otherwise treatment will be, that depends on how you react to the drugs they give you, but I must add that some women, who already have children of their own, actually volunteer to do it for the purposes of egg donation. So it can't be that bad, can it?"

"I don't know. You tell me."

He pursed his lips momentarily. "I don't know what regime of drugs they use at Catcott Manor, although I don't imagine it will much differ from ours."

"What is your regime?"

"Buserelin, by nasal spray for two weeks to calm the ovaries, followed by one to two weeks of Perganol to stimulate them, administered daily by deep intramuscular injection into the muscle of the buttock."

"Ouch! Sounds more like purgatory."

He grinned appreciatively. "Depends on who's wielding the needle, Sister."

I found myself grinning back. "Then what?"

"A single injection of Profasi to induce ovulation, given thirty-five hours before egg collection. The timing is critical, so the injection is usually given in the middle of the night."

"What are the side effects? Not very pleasant, as I remember."

"Not altogether, no, although it varies considerably from

person to person. Buserelin produces menopausal-like symptoms: hot flushes, night sweats, loss of libido . . ."

"Well, I think I can live with that."

"Also nausea, headache, increase in weight, increase in breast size and tenderness," Marcus, to his credit, shifted and wriggled uncomfortably, "fatigue, dizziness and mood changes, including depression and nervousness. But that's the worst any of my patients have had to put up with."

"That's bad enough, and they have an incentive. What about the other drugs?"

"Perganol isn't too bad, in fact, it often alleviates the Buserelin side effects. Profasi can cause similar effects to Buserelin, but for a shorter time."

"Then what?"

"Here in my clinic, the eggs are collected by ultrasound, which, as I said earlier, only requires local anaesthesia."

"Although Catcott Manor used laparoscopy on Mrs Murrell, which requires a general anaesthetic."

"I can only assume that was an exception."

"I certainly hope so. Then what?"

"The eggs are taken to the laboratory and fertilised by the addition, or in your case, the microinjection of sperm. They're then incubated and a check kept on their growth. When they reach the four-cell stage, they're replaced into the womb."

I looked at Marcus. "That's the bit I really don't like. Whatever else I may agree to, I want a tablet of stone guarantee that we'll be finished before any eggs can be replaced in me."

Marcus looked at the Prof. "What's the time scale, Professor? How much time will that give Mr Jones to investigate?"

"That depends on the clinic. Private clinics tend to keep patients in for longer, to justify their charges, and from what we've heard, Catcott is no exception." He turned back to me. "You'd probably go in two days before the eggs were collected. Tell them you're nervous and must have your husband with you – that won't be a problem. Replacement, in Catcott's case, is three to four days after collection, so that gives you at least three clear days before you have to get out. Will that be enough?"

Marcus looked at Tom, who said, "I would think so."

Prof said, "They may offer to have you overnight before commencement of treatment, for examinations. I would strongly advise against that, since it risks them discovering there's nothing wrong with either of you. The whole point of my involvement is to provide you with recent medical evidence which will obviate the need for that."

"Who would be giving me all these injections?" I asked. "The clinic?"

"Not necessarily. We could, if you're not staying too far away. Or your GP's nurse."

"In that case, do I really need to go through with them?"

"I'm afraid so, they'd know straight away at the clinic if you hadn't. You see, after the first week of injections, you'd have to have a daily scan to check how the follicles were developing. With this regime, they'd expect to see eight at least, rather than the one or two you'd normally have."

"Who does the scanning?"

"Again, we could at first, but the clinic will want to do it after a week, so that they can judge the best moment to collect the eggs. Miss Farewell," he continued quickly, "there is another thing."

"Yes?"

"Have you ever had a laparoscopy?"

"No, I haven't. Why?"

"You would have had an exploratory one before treatment here, and Catcott will notice the absence of a scar."

"Oh . . ."

"It's not a problem. I can give you a scar with stitch marks, but if you're in a hurry, I'll have to do it today, since it'll take a couple of weeks to heal properly."

The silence was broken by Marcus.

The Gift

"Professor, if I could have a few words with Miss Farewell alone in the corridor, I think we can resolve this now."

Prof looked at me. "Sister?"

"Very well." I got up and followed Marcus out. He spoke to me in a low voice.

"Tom told me about your financial problems."

"He had no right!"

"Perhaps not, but after that, and what I've just heard, I'll make sure you get your ten thousand."

I met his eyes. "I don't much like what I've heard either, Marcus. Do I get my guarantee that no eggs are replaced?"

"Of course."

I hesitated. "I just want to ask the Professor one question, then I'll decide."

It was his turn to hesitate. "All right," he said at last.

"Professor," I said when we were back inside, "there was something I wanted to ask you."

"Yes?"

"I'm sorry if this seems an impertinence, but what was it that made you change you mind about helping us?"

He gave his wry smile, then put his palms together and brought his fingertips almost prayer-like to his lips.

"You'll have to bear with me." A pause, then he spoke slowly, "I've devoted twenty-five years to working on the problems of infertility. One of the best days of my life was the twenty-fifth of July 1978, when Louise Brown, the first test-tube baby was born, even though I wasn't directly concerned. Why? I think the answer to that lies is in the words of the journalist Barbara Amiel, who wrote in *The Times* about when she was told she would be unable to have a child." He closed his eyes for a moment and then quoted, "'As the doctor spoke, all I could see was a large black crow sitting on her shoulder. The crow just sat there, its beak hard and yellow, ready to gnaw out my insides . . .'" He looked up at us. "There are plenty of people, usually those who have children of their own, who think that childless women should be able

33

to put up with large black crows. I don't happen to agree. I want to shoot them.

"Despite misgivings, the public have, by and large, accepted IVF. However, it does seem to me now that technology is beginning to outstrip ethics. We have women of fifty-nine having twins, and in places like California, the spectre of designer babies. We have the head of a gender clinic in London, who stands to make a great deal of money out of it, claiming that it's a basic human right to choose the sex of your baby. A basic human right? What would a woman watching her child starving to death in Africa make of that, I wonder? And now we have the revolting suggestion that ovarian tissue from aborted female foetuses should be used to give childless couples children. Does this mean that in the future babies will be conceived for this purpose, I wonder? This sort of publicity will cause a public backlash eventually and our work, *my* work, will be curtailed. There will be more large black crows sitting on women's shoulders. That's why, at first, I was instinctively against your investigation – I was afraid of what you might find. And that's why I've now changed my mind."

Five

I agreed, of course.

The Professor handed us both booklets explaining the fertility techniques used at his clinic and containing forms for us to fill in.

"These are what all prospective patients in this clinic are given," he said. "Answer the questions truthfully – it'll help me with your medical notes. We can alter anything that might go against you later."

"How long will it take you to prepare them?" asked Marcus.

"Two or three days. But I'll send a preliminary letter off to Dr Kent today."

After that, he took me into a side room where he administered a local anaesthetic, then with a scalpel, he made an incision low in my belly about two millimetres deep by ten long. He then put in a couple of stitches and applied a dressing.

"I'll take the stitches out when I see you on Friday," he said.

I hadn't felt a thing.

We were on the point of leaving when he said suddenly to Marcus, "What is it you think they're up to at Catcott, Mr Evans?"

"Your guess is as good as mine," Marcus replied. "Possibly better. For what it's worth. I think the suggestion raised earlier is as likely as any – that they're charging people a lot of money for having their own children, then using donor sperm."

"Hmm. Risky, since it could be proved by DNA testing."

"Some variation on that theme, then. Whatever it is, I'm sure money's at the bottom of it. It usually is."

The Prof said, "A technique that's used by some clinics with men who find it difficult to come to terms with their infertility is to mix donor and patient sperm together, so that there's always an element of doubt. Let me have a look at any contract they give you and I'll go over it to check for any let out clauses along those lines hidden in the small print."

With that, he showed us out.

"Strange man," mused Tom as the taxi pulled away. "Obsessive, almost."

"Dedicated," I corrected him. I'd rather taken to the Professor.

Marcus, ever the diplomat, said, "Perhaps you have to be slightly obsessive to achieve the necessary dedication."

Back in his office, we started on the preliminaries.

"I'll phone your line manager tomorrow and sort out your leave," he said to me. "Is it still Miss Whittington?"

"No, she's moved on. It's a Mrs Compton now." I gave him her extension number.

"Fine." He made a note. "I'll arrange it in principle and give her the specific dates when we know more." He looked up. "You shouldn't need too much time off before your first appointment with the clinic, probably not until you start the medication."

"Hopefully, not even then," I said.

He smiled. "Indeed. But to be on the safe side, we'd better book it from then. Now, what shall we have as name and address?"

"It has to be in London," said Tom. "For us to have had treatment at St Michael's, and also to be reasonably handy for Catcott. As for name, we might as well use mine. It does have the advantage of verisimilitude."

"Jo Jones," I said experimentally. "It doesn't sound right, somehow."

"You could make it Josie," Tom said.

"No, stick to what you're familiar with," said Marcus. "Jo most of the time, Josephine when you use it with Jones. It'll help you remember."

"Josephine Jones," I repeated. "Still doesn't sound right."

"You don't marry someone for their name," Tom said.

"As to the address," Marcus continued, "I know one of our staff flats becomes free at the end of the week, I'll make sure it stays free."

I stared at him. "You mean we're actually going to have a real address?"

"Oh yes. By sod's law, it would be the thing that gave you away if you didn't. Don't worry," he said, seeing my expression, "you're not going to have to live there."

"Where is it?" asked Tom.

"Lambeth. Not far from your old place."

"What about phone calls?"

"I'll have them redirected here to an answerphone. The same for any mail."

"If we're going in for this amount of detail," I said, "what about jobs? I take it I've got one."

"If I remember rightly, you used to work at the Royal United in Birmingham, didn't you?"

"Yes?"

"Well, that's where you met Tom. He can be some sort of computer expert who travels round the country."

"Computer Systems Analyst," Tom said succinctly.

"Yes, that sounds vapid enough. You met Jo there – ah, shall we say three years ago?"

"Four," said Tom. "We married a year later and Jo moved here. We tried for kids for two years, like the Professor said, we were on a waiting list for six months, and now we've been having treatment for six months."

Marcus was noting this all down.

"Where am I working now?" I asked.

"Off work while being treated, I suggest," said Marcus. "I

can get you on to the payroll of any hospital in London, but we don't want them phoning up and asking for you."

"So where was my last job?"

"St Christopher's. I know the personnel officer there. Nursing Sister?"

"I'd suggest not," I said. "If they are up to something at the clinic, they won't want clients with any medical knowledge there."

"Good point. I'd prefer it to be something within the NHS, though."

"Medical secretary?" suggested Tom. "That's the sort of person I'd have been likely to meet."

Marcus grunted his agreement and scribbled.

"Why are we living in a flat in Lambeth?" I asked. "I mean, with our joint incomes, and the fact that we want children and can afford all this treatment."

"We've got a house lined up," said Tom after a pause, "and we found a buyer for our old place. The housing market's still pretty awful, so we sold up while we had the chance and took the flat temporarily."

"Good, good," murmured Marcus, getting it all down.

"What about a GP?" I asked. "They're bound to want to know who our doctor is."

"Mine'll agree," Tom said. "He has before."

"Very obliging of him."

"Isn't it?"

"Is there anything else we need to think of at this stage?" Marcus asked.

"We need to find out about the security system at Catcott," Tom said.

"I'll speak to Miles. Anything else?"

"Do we inform the local police?" Tom spoke again.

"I'd rather avoid it if possible. It nearly always makes trouble."

"What about general things," I asked. "Place of birth, next of kin and so on?"

"The truth. I don't see why either of you need alter your histories for before you met, although perhaps you'd better think it through in case there are any problems."

We talked around it for a while longer until I said it was time for me to leave to catch my train. Marcus phoned for a taxi and Tom waited with me downstairs for it to arrive.

"I'm glad you agreed," he said awkwardly, after a pause. "Couldn't really imagine doing it with anyone else."

I smiled. That was quite an admission for him. I said, "Marcus seems to be going to an awful lot of trouble over this, for what might not be a very serious crime."

"I'd have said murder was quite serious, wouldn't you?"

"But as you said earlier, it'll never be proved. And people do die of post-op infection, you know."

"She was murdered, Jo. I'm sure of it."

I nodded slowly. Tom's an ex-policeman and can almost smell murder.

"But there is another reason Marcus is keen on it," he continued. "He and Ashby knew each other before this and apparently, the people at ReMLA have been worried for some time about the way things are going."

"Technology outstripping ethics, you mean?"

"Yes. And the BMA's recent approval of the proposal to use aborted foetuses in fertility treatment was the last straw for a lot of them. They decided to take a tougher line, and when this came up, Ashby came straight round to Marcus."

"So this morning's meeting was a set-up to get Professor Fulbourn involved."

"I think that might be overstating it a bit."

At this point the taxi drew up outside. Tom came out with me.

"Jo," he said as he opened the door, "sorry about what I said in the pub. Just me putting things clumsily."

In other words, I thought as the taxi pulled away, you aren't sorry about what you said, just the way you said it.

The stitches in my belly had started to itch.

*   *   *

Work the next day seemed other-worldish, an irrelevance almost, and I went through the motions on autopilot until Mrs Compton, my Nursing Officer, came to see me.

"I've had a phone call from a Mr Evans at the Department of Health," she said in her no-nonsense Scottish accent when we were in my office, "requesting that you be given sabbatical leave. A little bit iron-fist-in-velvet-glove, your Mr Evans, isn't he?" She was a comfortably built woman in her forties with greying hair and a pleasant, square face.

"Yes, he is rather."

"He wouldn't give me any details, just said you could assist with an investigation. Not as in help us with our enquiries, I hope?"

I laughed. "No, nothing like that. You remember the serial killer we had here last year?"*

"Do I not!"

"Well, Mr Evans was in charge of the DoH investigation. It so happens that I'm in a position to help him with another."

"Not a similar one, I trust? I wouldn't want to have to look for your replacement just yet."

"No, nothing like that," I said again, hoping it was the truth.

I couldn't give her exact dates, but I showed her how cover could be arranged and promised her accurate details as soon as I had them.

After she'd gone, I stayed in my office a few minutes, staring out into the Duty Room with its bustling occupants. Mrs Compton's visit had brought reality home to me and I was scared. Working with patients as I did, I had more reason than most to know how vulnerable anybody in any hospital bed is.

On Friday, I was back in London, meeting Tom at St Michael's

* *The Ladies of the Vale*

so that Professor Fulbourn could remove my stitches and go through our medical histories with us. He was looking a bit happier, although we didn't find out why until later.

"I've been through the forms you filled in for me, and compiled your medical notes accordingly." He looked over the top of his glasses at us. "You're sure that all the information is accurate? You, Mr Jones, have never had torsion of a testicle, for instance?"

"I hope not."

"And they descended properly at birth?"

"Er, I think so."

"I'll check before you go; it's the sort of thing they'd spot immediately at Catcott. And you, Miss Farewell, have never had a termination?"

"No."

"Good. I notice you both smoke," he continued. "They won't like that, so I've said in the notes that you've both given up." He looked up at us again. "So perhaps you'd better – for a while, anyway. You don't want to be caught out on that."

"We both smoke so little that we didn't think it would matter," Tom said.

"Ten cigarettes a day can halve a woman's chance of conception," Prof said severely. "It also depresses sperm count. And your drinking's a bit on the high side, Mr Jones. They'd definitely disapprove of that, so I've halved the amount and suggest you do the same. Now, I'd like you both to go through these." He handed us each a file. "Your medical notes. Check them now, please, for any discrepancies, then keep the photocopies I've made for reference."

"You want us to memorise them?" asked Tom.

"No, but it would be a good idea to remember the main points."

Tom grunted and started going through his and I did likewise.

Everything was there; referral from GP to local clinic and then to St Michael's; first interview; lab tests; medication,

41

treatment, failure. Times three. A sad story, had it been true. And at the end, "recommend AID", then, "? microinjection".

There was nothing in them to query or object to.

"Good," said the Professor. "I'll get them off as soon as you've gone."

"So soon?" said Tom.

"Yes," he sad, almost casually. "You see, I wrote to Dr Kent at Catcott as I said I would after I saw you on Tuesday, and she phoned me this morning. It would seem that we were right about the kind of case she favours, she says she's had a cancellation and would like to see you on Wednesday week at nine."

Six

Catcott Manor: warm stone and tile, creeper covered, dozing in the morning sun, high on Salisbury Plain. Tom parked the car (an Astra saloon, not his own Mini-Cooper) beside a line of others at the back of the building and switched off the engine.

"Ready?"

I nodded.

"Good." He touched my shoulder briefly, then opened his door. He was wearing a smart, though somewhat sharp, blazer and light-coloured trousers to fit his image of a salesman, which he'd decided might offer some advantages over a computer expert, while I was wearing a simple dress.

We walked slowly across the gravelled drive to the semicircle of steps that led up to the large front door, which stood open. We pushed through an inner door into a sizeable entrance hall, dim after the sunlight outside. An unoccupied desk stood opposite. We approached. There was a bellpush and a small notice: PLEASE RING FOR ATTENTION.

Tom glanced at me, then pushed his thumb firmly on to it. A bell trilled distantly. We looked around.

At one end of the hall was an open fireplace you could have walked into. Above it hung a picture, but the paint was too darkened to make out any detail. At the other end, the obligatory suit of armour looked too good to be true. A wide staircase with an ornate banister curved upwards.

Footsteps, then a pretty, fresh-faced girl with curly blonde hair appeared wearing a white coat.

"Hello, you must be Mr and Mrs Jones."

"That's right," Tom said.

"Would you like to take a seat?" She indicated some chairs next to the armour. "Dr Kent will see you shortly."

"Thank you," we both said, and made our way over. Tom sat next to the armour and examined it for a moment.

"Fake," he whispered to me.

I glanced up at the girl, but she was talking into the telephone. I tried to swallow my heartbeat, tried telling myself that this was how a genuine patient would feel. It didn't help much.

It had been a busy week. Marcus had wanted photos, my birth certificate and other documents from me, and I'd spent the first weekend at Tom and Holly's house, where he and I had gone over the fiction of our lives together *ad nauseam*. This turned out to be a good move *vis-à-vis* Holly. And to be honest it put my feelings about Tom into a better perspective, watching him with Holly and their son.

We had looked over the flat, our 'home' in Lambeth. It was frankly dingy, but Marcus swore he would arrange to have it made look homely. "Just in case," he said.

Marcus and Tom had wrestled with the problem of obtaining plans of the clinic's security system from the firm that had installed it.

"They refused to tell us a damned thing until we got a court order," said Marcus.

"Claimed their first duty was to their customer." said Tom.

They were both quite indignant.

The last weekend, I spent with my mother. I'd debated whether or not to tell her what I was doing, and decided not. She'd worry, she'd want to know why, which, if I told her, would only make her feel guilty.

I decided to be an orphan.

Tuesday evening and night, I stayed with Tom and Holly again, because of our early start in the morning. Holly tried to treat it all as a joke, but you could see that she was worried. She and me both.

The phone on the receptionist's desk buzzed and she picked it up.

"Mr and Mrs Jones," she called. "Dr Kent will see you now."

We followed her down a dim, panelled corridor. She stopped and knocked at a door.

"Come in."

We followed her in. A figure had risen from a desk and was coming across to us.

"Good morning Mrs Jones, Mr Jones." She took our hands in turn, her grip firm and steady. "I'm Dr Kent."

She was slightly taller than me, say five and a half feet, with a full figure that just stopped short of being bulky. She was wearing a light-grey skirt and a cream top, with a single rope of pearls round her neck. "Do come and sit down." She indicated chairs in front of her desk. "Thank you, Leila," she said over her shoulder, and the receptionist silently left.

She resumed her seat behind her desk. I noticed it was arranged so that the light from the window fell across her face, as it did across ours. Psychology to put us at ease, I thought, as was the fact that her seat was no higher than ours.

"I trust you had a good journey." Her face was square jawed, strongly featured and with very little make-up, framed by iron-grey hair cut in a bob.

"Fine thanks, doctor," Tom replied. "Not too bad once we were out of the metropolis."

"Good. Now I—"

"And we'd like to thank you for seeing us so soon. We're truly grateful, aren't we, Jo?"

"Yes." I said dutifully, cringing a little inside. His portrayal of a pushy London salesman was rather too accurate for comfort.

Dr Kent said smoothly. "As I told Professor Fulbourn, we

had a sudden cancellation and I like to make the best possible use of my time. Now, I have your notes here which Professor Fulbourn has sent me, but I hope you'll bear with me, while I ask some questions." Her voice was slightly deep for a woman's, but soft and educated. She turned to me.

"I see you've been married for three years. When did you first become worried about infertility."

Tom said. "Since we were married really, wouldn't you say, Jo?"

Dr Kent turned to him. "I'd prefer to hear Mrs Jones's answers first, if you wouldn't mind, Mr Jones." She smiled to take the sting out of it, although the smile didn't reach her eyes. "I'll come back to you in a moment."

"Oh. Sorry, I'm sure."

"That's quite all right. Mrs Jones?" She had rather piercing grey eyes, I noticed, and her face, which was unlined, seemed to be younger somehow than her body, so that it was difficult to guess her age.

"Not long after our marriage, as Tom said," I replied. "We both wanted children, so we stopped using contraceptives and I was surprised when I didn't become pregnant."

"Why were you surprised? It can sometimes take a long time."

"I've always been very regular and never had any trouble that way. I was certain I would become pregnant quickly."

"I notice you've never used the contraceptive pill."

"No. I – er—" I glanced at Tom and felt myself redden slightly, "I preferred the cap."

She glanced down at the notes again. "Well, it would seem that Professor Fulbourn's investigations bear out your feelings."

"Yes," I said simply.

"So, to sum up your history, you went to your GP a year after you were married, but he didn't refer you for a further year. You then went firstly to – er—" she checked the file in front of her, "St Martin's for fertility tests, and subsequently to St Michael's to try *in vitro* fertilisation. Would that be a fair summing up?"

"Yes."

"This last six months must have been very distressing for you." Statement, not question, and said with real sincerity.

"Yes, it has been."

"I'm sure." She turned to Tom. "I notice you've been married before, Mr Jones. You didn't have some inkling of the problem then?"

"My first wife didn't want children, so the problem never came up."

"I see. So when did you first begin to worry, Mr Jones?"

"About the same time as Jo, really. It was me who suggested she should go to the doctor's for a check up."

"You assumed that the problem was with her?"

"Yes, I did," he said defensively. "I thought at the time it was nearly always the woman—"

"Whereas you now realise that that's not the case at all."

"No," he mumbled. "Prof Fulbourn told us."

"Mr Jones, this must have been very painful for you as well. Nobody, least of all me, wishes to cast aspersions on your virility. It has always seemed ridiculous to me that what is essentially a medical problem should reflect on a man's maleness." This was said sincerely as well, but part of me wondered whether it was really the best approach.

"That's what I've always told you, Tom." I said, playing the part.

"Yeah. Yes, you have."

"I notice you've been offered AID. Donor insemination."

"That's right. But I – *we* – wanted our own child. Didn't we, Jo?"

"Yes, we did," I said, still the dutiful wife. Then I looked at him and added quickly. "But it would have been our own child, Tom, I . . ."

"Well, it's possible we can help you," Dr Kent interposed quickly. "Not definite by any means, but certainly possible.

47

Now, the first thing we need," she continued crisply, "is a sample of your sperm, Mr Jones. Only that way can we tell. Obviously, you're familiar with this procedure?"

Tom nodded dumbly.

"And it has been at least three days since you last ejaculated, but no more than seven?"

"That's right, yes."

"Then I suggest that I quickly examine you now, and then, while you're producing your sample, I can examine Mrs Jones."

She stood up and crossed to some screens. "If you'd just like to come behind here please, Mr Jones."

Funny, the proprieties we observe, I thought as Tom disappeared from view. Except for his shoes, twinkling beneath the screens.

A muted instruction, then his trousers flopped over his ankles. He coughed.

Two minutes later, he emerged, rather red faced.

"I'll show you the cubicle now," Dr Kent said, and he sheepishly followed her out.

A moment later, she came back into the room. "Would you like to come through here, Mrs Jones?"

She led me through a connecting door to a bright, well-equipped examination room. A space-age scanner glowed beside the bed.

"I'll leave you while you undress," she said. "Just from the waist down, please. Then, perhaps you'd wait on the bed."

My heart began beating against my ribs again. Would Fulbourn's false scar stand up to examination? He'd sworn it would. Perhaps she'd find something we hadn't thought of, something I didn't know about?

I'd been on the bed less than a minute when she came back in.

"You're ready? Good. Could you put your feet up in the stirrups, please?"

She helped me place my ankles in widely spaced supports above the bed.

Just as well I've done this before, I thought. It's probably the most undignified posture possible for a woman to adopt. She picked up the speculum.

Adopt? That's the trouble, the stirrups make you feel trapped, defenceless, open to violation . . .

"Try to relax please, Mrs Jones."

"I'm sorry. I've never been able to get used to this."

"Few people are. Try to think about something else – the end result, perhaps . . ."

I thought of Harry Jones, and curiously, it seemed to work.

"That's better." A moment later, she continued, "Is there anything else you'd like to tell me, in addition to the infor-mation in your notes?" Good psychology to ask me now, when we weren't face to face.

"I don't think so, no."

"No venereal disease of any kind, problems you'd rather your husband didn't know about?"

"No, nothing like that."

"Please forgive me for asking. It's something we have to check."

"Of course."

"Well, everything seems to be fine here," she said a few moments later. The speculum was withdrawn and she helped me to lower my feet.

"Your husband – I have the impression that he's had some difficulty in coming to terms with his condition." She lay a towel across my midriff. "Stay where you are a moment please, I want to do a quick scan."

"It's true about my husband," I said, glad of the oppor-tunity to say something about Tom. "He's a very socia-ble man, an extrovert, one of the lads – it hit him very hard."

"I can see that."

"He tries to cover it up."

"I can see that, too. Has there been pressure on him – on both of you – to start a family."

"We neither of us have parents still alive," I said carefully, "but there has been pressure. Peer pressure." I hesitated, drew in a breath. "I think the worst moment was when we were out with some friends one evening. They'd had a few drinks and one of them said, 'When are you going to start producing then, Tom? I thought you were a family man.' "

I shook my head. "He bluffed it out, but it was all I could do to persuade him to stay afterwards."

"I can see how it would hurt a man like him. I'm just going to put some jelly on your tummy . . ." she squeezed some on to me from a plastic container, then, "Does he enjoy his work? He's a salesman, I believe?"

"Yes, he sells medical equipment and he's very good at it, very successful." I smiled wanly. "That's how come we can afford all this treatment."

"So having a family is important to him?"

"It's important to us both, doctor."

She smiled. "I'm sure it is, Mrs Jones. Now, let's find out what we can see with this."

She applied the sensor to my abdomen, slid it around experimentally for a moment, then moved it more purposefully while she studied the screen. "Ye-es, it all appears to be as Professor Fulbourn noted . . . now, try to keep very still, please, I want to take some measurements." She delicately manipulated the sensor until one of my ovaries was in the middle of the picture, then expanded the image until it filled the screen. It was in colour and the detail was the best I'd ever seen. She pressed a button on the sensor and a cross appeared on the screen, which she manoeuvred to one end of the ovary – then my stomach grumbled and the image shook.

"Try to keep still, please."

"Sorry."

She placed further crosses and read off the measurements from the digital display on the panel.

"Well," she said at last, "everything seems to be satisfactory here." She removed the sensor and handed me another towel.

"So you won't need to do another laparoscopy?"

"From what I've seen, I'm sure we can accept Professor Fulbourn's findings. If you'd like to get dressed now, I'll go back to my office and see if your husband is ready. Would you like to come through when you're ready?"

"Er, yes."

"Good. No need to hurry." She replaced the sensor on the machine and left.

I took a breath. So far so good? I hoped so. I wiped the jelly from my abdomen and slowly got dressed.

Tom was in the office with her when I got back.

"Please sit down, Mrs Jones. Your husband's sample has already gone to the laboratory."

She waited until I was seated before continuing.

"As I told you both earlier, I can't say definitely whether we can treat you or not until I have the laboratory results."

"How long will that take?" Tom.

"About a week. Now—"

"And how much is it going to cost us?"

She looked at him a moment before replying. "I can't give you an exact figure until I've seen the laboratory results, but it will be between three and four thousand pounds."

"I see. Half payable before treatment and half after?"

"No. If we agree to treat you, we would require the full amount before you actually came to stay here. But you're jumping ahead rather, Mr Jones. I was about to say something about microinjection. It's a very new technique, although having said that, we have already had some success with it. Success or failure will depend on the quality of your sperm – if our investigations show that your sperm is unlikely to fertilise your wife's ova, then we would be charlatans if we accepted your money and—"

"But surely," interrupted Tom, "if it was good enough for

51

Prof Fulbourn to attempt IVF, then it'll be worth trying with microinjection."

She looked at him with barely concealed dislike. "There is a strong likelihood that that will be the case, but until we've completed our tests, I cannot commit myself. There is a further point. I notice that you both used to smoke, but gave it up when treatment started. I trust that is still the case?"

Tom looked down at his hands. "Didn't think it would make any difference, not after Prof Fulbourn told us we'd have to use a donor."

"Well, it can make a difference, a big difference. I hope that's understood."

He looked quickly up at her. "Yes, doctor."

"Good." She smiled again. "I suggest that you have your blood samples taken now, then go home and try not to worry."

"That's easier said than done," Tom, gloomily.

Dr Kent stood up. "True, but try nevertheless." She escorted us to the door. "Goodbye, and good luck!"

We looked at each other but didn't say anything as we walked back to the entrance hall. Leila was waiting for us by her desk.

"Blood samples," she said brightly. "Who's going first? Mrs Jones?"

"No, Mr Jones," I said firmly, propelling Tom forward. He had this thing about blood (his brother had been a haemophiliac) and he tended to feel faint at the sight of it. With a glance back at me, he followed Leila into the cubicle.

"Don't you like needles?" I heard her ask.

"Not that," he replied gruffly. "Can't stand the sight of blood."

"Why don't you close your eyes, then?"

Why hadn't I thought of that? I wondered.

It was just as we were saying goodbye to Leila that a huge hulking figure in uniform emerged from a passageway, saw us, grunted and quickly withdrew. I had just enough time to register the lantern jaw and close-set eyes in the slab of a face. There was something familiar about it.

"Ye gods!" Tom said in a stage whisper to Leila. "Who was that? Jaws?"

She laughed. "No, that was Cal, our security guard."

"Cal?"

She leaned forward conspiringly. "Short for Caliban." She laughed again. "But it's not his real name, so don't tell him I said it."

Seven

"I wonder what his real name is," Tom said as we drove back up through the parkland that surrounded the manor and through the gate. "Maybe Ashby can tell us."

"Caliban certainly suited him." I withdrew a cigarette from my pack and deliberately lit it. "Tom, don't you think your ignorant loudmouth act with Dr Kent was a bit OTT?"

He grinned. "It's what comes naturally."

"I'm not joking. She took a dislike to you, and I can't say I blame her."

"She'll still take us on as patients, though."

"How can you know that?"

He took a breath and let it out. "Let's suppose for a moment she was worried enough by the Murrell incident and the ReMLA enquiry to be on the look-out for a plant — what's the last thing she'd suspect?"

"I know what you're—"

"I'll tell you anyway — a fully paid up member of the loudmouth tendency. She may dislike me, but she won't suspect me."

"OK, but she might not *want* a member of the loudmouth tendency as a patient."

"But from what Professor Fulbourn told us, we're just the combination she's looking for — fertile woman and infertile man. She wants us as patients all right, why else would she have had us down here so quickly?"

"She may have had a genuine cancellation, they do happen."

54

"Surely there would have been someone further up the queue than us. No, Fulbourn got it right: we fulfil the criteria she wants."

"All right." I drew on my cigarette to conceal my own irritation with him. "I still can't understand why you had to be quite so . . . objectionable."

"Because it creates a credible character that gets under her guard, and will also be an explanation for my nosiness later on, that's why. And now," he said, "if you don't mind, I want to indulge in a little nostalgia."

I gave up. After a short silence, I said, "Why nostalgia?"

"I was stationed here when I was in the army."

"I'd forgotten you were in the army," I said slowly. "How long were you in for?"

"Three years. Half a lifetime ago."

"Did you enjoy it? You said nostalgia."

"I did and I didn't. Probably seems better in retrospect. I don't regret it though."

"No." I looked at him, thinking: the services leave an indelible mark on whomever they touch. I'd seen it so often before in patients – a toughness, an independence, a stoicism, but also sometimes a bloody-mindedness and plain bloody ignorance.

I stubbed my cigarette and looked out of the window. We must have been in the middle of the plain. It stretched away as far as you could see on all sides, dotted with patchy scrub; undulating, like a carpet that's been laid on rocky ground, its rough grass pile a vivid green.

"Tom, stop a minute."

He glanced at me, then pulled in to the side of the narrow road.

"What is it?"

"Look." I pointed. "Cowslips."

"Oh, yes. I can't remember when I last saw that many."

The ground on my side was thick with them, their bright yellow flowers studding the coarse grass like jewels.

"Neither can I, they're not so common now." I opened the door.

"Careful, there might be unexploded shells. It's not an army training ground for nothing."

"Not this close to a public road, surely?"

"Probably not, no. But don't go too far."

I got out and walked a few paces, and after a moment, he joined me.

The air was an elixir: soft, not cold, but cool enough to be a foil for the warm sun and filled with streamers of birdsong.

"Skylarks," said Tom, pointing to where one hung in the blue above us. He grinned at me. "Just think, if it wasn't for the army, all this would have all been ploughed up years ago by some farmer. No cowslips, no skylarks. God, this brings back memories."

We stood there in silence, thinking our different thoughts. I was thinking: maybe it's the stress . . . they say that danger sharpens the senses, maybe that's why I'm feeling all this so intensely. At that moment, I wished he could have put his arm around me, but I'd stayed in his house with his wife and that was the one thing he couldn't do.

We drove down to Salisbury, where Tom had arranged to collect plans of the manor from the Planning Records Department and to visit Combes, the firm that had installed the security system.

Salisbury was rather like Latchvale, only more so, if you see what I mean. Similar narrow streets and timbered buildings, but bigger, on a more expansive scale, and somehow more aloof. The lancet spire of the cathedral dominated the whole city, unlike the more homely Ladies of Latchvale.

We found a pub, a time-warp called the Haunch of Venison opposite the Poultry Cross, where we had lunch. Tom wanted to know in detail everything that had passed between Dr Kent and myself. I told him, then said. "If you didn't know there was something wrong with the place, you'd never suspect it."

He snorted. "Speak for yourself. It's obvious she's nothing but a suppressed dyke."

"Oh, come on. I bet you say that about all successful independent women."

"Not at all. I've never said it about you, have I?"

"That's different."

"In what way?" he asked innocently.

"I'm not rising to that one."

He smiled. "OK, I admit I was influenced by her appearance, but I say it mostly because of her obvious dislike of men. She—"

"Dislike of *you*, you mean."

"She's supposed to be a specialist in male infertility. yet she spent virtually all her time on you."

"Yes, and asked me a great many questions about you. Besides, it was elementary to check me out first. I'm the one who'd have to carry any baby."

"Ah yes, a women's lot."

"She may dislike you, and who can blame her, but I bet she spends more time on your sperm than she did on me."

He grinned and I realised he'd been deliberately winding me up.

"Very funny, smart-ass."

"Seriously Jo, if you think she's going to spend time on my sperm, you're assuming she's *bona fide*."

"It's not impossible."

He snorted again, then looked at his watch. "I'd better get over to the Planning Department. What are you going to do?"

"How long d'you think you'll be?"

"A couple of hours."

"I'll look round the town, maybe go to the cathedral."

"I'll meet you at the Poultry Cross in a couple of hours, then."

I wandered through the streets, guided by the tip of the spire until I passed through an ornate gatehouse to the close.

The cathedral was stunning. Stately, remote, even cold in its very perfection, it was like an iceberg floating in a sea of green. St Chad's in Latchvale was a cuddly baby in comparison.

Halfway across the close. I stopped beside a statue, a sculpture in bronze of the *Walking Madonna* by the late Dame Elizabeth Frink. But this madonna didn't just walk, she strode, stretching the fabric of the skirt that reached down to her ankles. Her face was gaunt, her jaw clenched in absolute determination, her eyes focused inwards. This Mother of Christ was totally absorbed, totally committed.

She was also quite sexless, and looking at her, I realised that Tom had been wrong about Dr Kent. She, too, was sexless.

The time flew by as I explored the cathedral and its surroundings and I arrived back at the Poultry Cross to find Tom smoking a cheroot and looking at his watch.

"Sorry," I said, not over sincerely. He'd had no qualms about leaving me for two hours. "Did you find what you wanted?"

"I think so. If you're quite ready, shall we go?"

We took the M3 back to London. Tom asked me to drive so that he could study the plans. We didn't talk much and when we'd reached the outskirts to London, I realised to my fury that he'd dozed off. I made him drive the rest of the way.

Marcus was in his office with Ashby when we got there. We told them what had happened, then Marcus asked Tom about the security system.

"Well, you were right about it being more sophisticated than warranted, Dr Ashby," Tom said. He laid the plans on Marcus' desk. "We caught a glimpse of the security guard you mentioned as well. Leila, the receptionist, referred to him as Caliban."

Ashby smiled. "Apt. His real name's Calvin Moore. He's an American. Don't be fooled by his appearance though, I sensed a considerable animal cunning."

"I'll bear that in mind."

"The point is, Tom," Marcus said, "will you be able to get round the system if you have to?"

"I hope so." He spread the plans over the desk and we poured over them.

"This is the ground floor," he said. "There are twenty external windows and two doors. The windows, which are sash, have vibration sensors, and the doors have magnetic reed contact switches."

"Explain," said Marcus.

"Vibration sensors are just that – any movement of the window and an alarm goes off. You'll have seen magnetic reed switches. Two small plastic plates, like this" – he held his hands with the palms parallel with each other – "are set flush in two surfaces, one in the door and one in the door frame. The one that moves when the door opens contains a magnet, and the other a switch, which is held in the off position so long as the magnet is close to it. As soon as the magnet moves away when the door opens, the switch is released and sets off the alarm."

Marcus nodded. "I've seen them. So that prevents anyone getting inside. But you'll already be inside, won't you?"

"Yes, but that's covered pretty effectively as well. There's a closed-circuit TV camera with a built-in passive infra-red sensor here in the hall, covering the main stairs" – he pointed – "and more infra-red sensors here, in Kent's office; here, in her deputy's office next to the laboratory; and also here, covering the back stairs."

"How do these infra-red sensor things work?"

"They send out an infra-red beam which detects any move-ment of heat, including from the human body. They're placed in a top corner, here" – he indicated again – "where the beam can cover the whole room."

"But only in those two rooms?"

"That's right, which would suggest that that's where any-thing useful to us is likely to be. And I did notice a fire safe in Kent's room."

Marcus studied the plan for a moment.

"I can see your problem," he said at last. "If you come down either of the stairs, you'll be seen or detected." He looked up. "What about the lift?"

"That has a magnetic reed switch as well."

"Hmm. So even if you made it downstairs without being detected, the moment you went into either Kent's office or her deputy's, the alarm'd go off."

"Just one alarm, in the security room, so it doesn't wake up the whole house."

"Why would that be?"

"Combes said Kent wanted it that way, so that a false alarm wouldn't wake up the patients."

"Bullshit – sorry, Jo."

"That's all right."

"Yes," said Tom. "What I think, and Combes agreed with me after we'd discussed it, is that this system looks as though its function is to safeguard against intruders, whereas in fact, it's just as effective against inside snoopers. No one can get downstairs at night without the security guard knowing, and even if they do, the infra-red sensors pick them up the moment they go into either Kent's or her deputy's room. I should have mentioned, the control panel in the security room also shows the guard exactly where the breach is, be it window, door, room, whatever."

Marcus absently scratched the dome of his head with a finger.

"No way to neutralise the system?"

"None. If we attempted to cut any of the wires, not that there are any showing anywhere, a general alarm goes off."

"Surely, the guard isn't in the security room twenty-four hours a day?"

"No, he isn't. But *any* interference with the control panel at any time also sets off a general alarm."

Marcus let out a sigh. "That only leaves drugging the guard." He looked up at Tom. "I'm being serious, as a last resort."

"Even that's covered. During the night, he has to key in a code every hour. If he doesn't, the general alarm goes off."

"Combes wouldn't tell you the code?"

"*Couldn't* tell me. It can be changed every night, if the guard feels like it."

"Does the same apply to the actual timing of when it's keyed in?"

"No, that's set on the hour."

"I see." He paused. "So is there anything you can do?"

"Oh, we'll have to do something – I can't think that we'll find out what they're up to without some snooping. There is one weakness in the system . . ."

"Well?"

"The closed-circuit TV camera plus infra-red sensor in the main hall. Kent apparently wanted it because it can be used during the day, but it has a blind spot."

"Where?"

"Here." He pointed to the landing at the top of the main stairs. "Because of the ornate design of the staircase, and the angle of the camera, it's possible, so Combes tell me, to lower oneself into the hall from the back of the top landing and get into the corridor behind without being seen."

"Can you use it?"

"I don't know yet. I'll have to think about it and have a better look next time we go down."

"When will that be?" asked Ashby.

"We've made a provisional appointment for today week."

"Assuming she wants to treat you," said Marcus.

"She will," said Tom. "For the reasons we've already gone into."

Marcus called a taxi for me shortly after this. It made me feel vaguely resentful having to leave them still discussing what intimately concerned me, and then I thought that maybe I was being paranoid – that was the problem of living so far away from the centre of planning.

"You won't have anything to worry about until next Wednesday," Marcus had assured me as I left.

I'd be glad when it came and I knew where I stood, and would be able to play a full part in the planning.

Marcus, however, was wrong. He rang me at work at twenty-past twelve on Monday.

"Jo, we've got a problem. Dr Kent has just left a message on the answerphone for the flat. She's in London on business and intends calling on you at three. I think it's essential that you're there in time to meet her."

Eight

"Marcus, it can't be done." I could hear the wail in my voice.

"It can, Jo, I've—"

"But what does it matter? We're just not at home, that's all."

"She knows you don't have a job."

"So what?"

"Jo, we don't know why she's calling, and we do need to know. It may be some kind of test. If she doesn't see you, it'll leave a question mark in her mind."

"But—"

"No more arguments, just listen. There's a train leaving New Street for London in forty minutes – a taxi should get you there in that time. Tom will be waiting for you at Euston and will get you to the flat."

"But what about . . . ?"

"Don't waste any more time, just go." The line clicked shut.

For a moment my mind was totally blank, then I cleared the line to phone for a taxi. There was a knock at my door. It was Mary. I beckoned her in.

"Are you all right, Jo?"

"Fine. I'm sorry, but I've got to go off for the afternoon. can you look after things?"

"Sure. Do you . . . ?"

The phone was answered. "Hello? I need a taxi to take me to Birmingham New Street . . . yes, and it's urgent, please . . . from the main entrance of the hospital."

63

"What is it, Jo? Bad news?"

"I'll tell you when I come back – OK?"

I went to my locker, thrust my 'civvies' into a plastic bag, grabbed my handbag and left. I joined the knot of smokers outside the main entrance (you're not supposed to smoke in the hospital). The taxi took an age and I'd just lit up myself when it appeared. I dropped the cigarette into the bin.

"Birmingham New Street, was it miss?"

"Yes. Can you do it in" – I looked at my watch – "twenty-nine minutes?"

"I can try."

And he did, I'll say that for him. I thrust him a ten pound note twenty-eight minutes later. There were queues at the ticket windows. Forty seconds to go. I ran over to the barrier past a line of shuffling people showing their tickets.

"Hey, miss!"

"I'll pay on the train, OK?"

"You'll have to buy a single."

Big deal. A whistle went as I clattered down the escalator. The train had just started to move as I yanked open the door and got a foot on the step. Someone's hands round my midriff gave me a push and I had the stray thought that any other time, this would be sexual harassment. The door slammed behind me. I found a seat and collapsed.

I waited until the ticket inspector came and paid the single fare (stares from other passengers, irrational feelings of guilt), then went to the loo and changed.

Once I'd recovered my breath and thought about it, I could see Marcus's point.

It might not count against us if Dr Kent couldn't find me and I phoned her later, but it would be so much better if she did and could see that what we'd said about ourselves was true. I wondered what it was she wanted and worried about what I would say. Wasn't it somewhat unprofessional for her to call on me like this? – although I'd seen my share of unprofessional consultants. Then I began to worry about the flat – would it look sufficiently like a home? I couldn't believe Tom or Marcus capable of making it look homely.

Well, Josephine. I thought, you can certainly forget any feelings of guilt over the money they're paying you. Curiously, this made me feel slightly better for a while, although by the time we were pulling into Euston, that feeling had evaporated and I was feeling worse than ever.

Tom was waiting at the gate.

"What about the flat?" I gabbled at him. "What about tea and coffee and—"

"All taken care of." He took my arm and, half walking, half running, led me over to the waiting car.

He'd obviously spoken to the driver, because we shot off before the door had even slammed shut. On the back seat was a bag containing oddments of shopping.

I looked at my watch. Two thirty-five. "We'll never make it," I said.

Tom shrugged. "We might not," he said. "But then again, we might."

"A fiver says we will," said the driver over his shoulder.

"You get paid enough already," Tom told him. Then he added diplomatically, "All right, I'll think about it."

The driver grunted, then concentrated on his driving. The engine revved and a taxi hooted as he swung across it.

I said after a few minutes, "What does she want, Tom? I can't understand why she should call on me like this."

"I don't know, but," he lowered his voice, "whatever it is, it could make or break this operation."

"Is that supposed to make me feel any better?"

"Waterloo bridge," Tom said. "That's halfway."

"It's a quarter to," I said.

The muddy banks of the river gleamed glutinously – I'd forgotten the Thames was tidal.

"Tom, what if she knows . . . realises I'm a plant while we're there?"

"Don't worry about that, the flat's wired and we won't be far away."

We grumbled to a halt. Minutes passed. Tom looked over the driver's shoulder, then at his watch.

"Sorry guv, snarl up at the lights."

"OK, we'll have to walk the rest—"

"Hang about."

The car on our left had edged forward, he swung quickly through the gap before the next car could take its place and into a side road. Right, right again and back on to the main road. Waterloo Station. More streets.

Tom said, "Pull in over—"

"Tom, it's *her*!" I'd seen her come out of the flats and walk away from us.

"Get down, Jo," Tom said. "Bernie, next left, then stop. Got that?"

"Right, guv'ner."

"Jo, as soon as we've stopped, get out and walk back up that road – that way you can't miss her."

"All right."

We slewed round the corner.

"And don't forget your shopping."

"And my handbag. Tom! The keys to the flat?"

We screeched to a halt.

"They're in your bag. Now *go*. And good luck."

I stumbled on the pavement as I got out, recovered and set off up the road, shopping in one hand, handbag over my shoulder. Turned the corner and saw her ahead, warning a matching grey skirt and jacket.

I suddenly realised how much better it would be if she spotted me rather than vice versa. There was a clothes shop to my right. I moved over to it, across the flow of pedestrians, across her path, and stopped in front of it . . .

It hadn't worked, I'd have to go after her . . . I'd never be seen dead in these clothes anyway.

"Mrs Jones?"

I turned. "Dr Kent? Hello, what a coincidence!" Don't overdo it . . .

"Not entirely, Mrs Jones, I've just called at your flat to see you. In fact, I left a message on your phone earlier."

"I haven't been in since this morning, I was just going back now. Er . . ." I hesitated, "did you say you'd called to see me?"

"I did. Would you mind very much if I came back to your flat now for a few minutes?"

"No, of course not." I hesitated again. "Is it bad news?"

"Not entirely." She looked round at the milling crowds. "But I'd prefer not to talk about it here."

"No. Well it's just up here." We began walking. "I can't believe you came up to London just to see us."

She smiled. "Well, no. I came for a conference. This afternoon's sessions are frankly dire, so I thought I'd take this opportunity for a domiciliary visit."

"That was . . . very kind of you – it's in here." I led the way into the block. "There's no lift, I'm afraid, but it's only on the next floor. Sorry, you know that already."

We began climbing.

She said. "Your husband mentioned that this was only temporary accommodation?"

"We're buying a house in Mitcham." I smiled, wryly. "Much more suitable for children."

"Yes."

"Just here." I fumbled in my bag for the key.

"Would you like me to hold your shopping?"

"That's all right, here it is."

For a horrible moment, I thought the key wasn't going to fit, then it did and the door swung open. I led her into the sitting room, trying to keep the surprise from my face. The flat had been transformed – it looked and smelt fresh, there was china on the sideboard, books in the bookcase and a vase of flowers and, from the top of the TV, an ostentatious wedding photo grinned down at us – how the hell had they managed that?

"Er – please sit down, Dr Kent. Would you like some tea or coffee?"

"Tea would be nice, but . . . ?" It was her turn to hesitate, "I'd also quite like the bathroom."

"It's just down there. The loo's separate."

"Thank you."

The loo paper had run out when I was last here – had they replaced it . . .?

I took the shopping into the kitchen and dumped it on the table. Where was the kettle? Small mercy she wasn't here to see me hunt for it – ah!

Filled it, plugged it in, found the teapot, thrust in a couple of bags. Sugar bowl, plate for biscuits. Heard her go back into the sitting room. Thank God she hadn't come in here . . . jug for milk . . .

The kettle boiled. I found a tray, loaded the tea things and took it through and smiled at her as I put it down. They couldn't have overlooked the loo paper could they?

Damage limitation.

"Would you like to help yourself, Dr Kent? Just need the bathroom myself a minute."

Loo paper! Thank God! Wouldn't have to make any excuses. I operated the flush, rinsed my hands and went back.

She put down her cup and said, "I'd better tell you why I'm here."

I poured myself some tea. My hands were shaking, but that didn't matter.

"We've looked very carefully at your husband's sperm, and I have to say that it presents something of a challenge."

"Oh." So Prof had overcooked it. "Oh dear."

"I'm not surprised that Professor Fulbourn failed with IVF – in fact, I'm rather surprised that a specialist with his reputation should have tried as many times with it as he did."

I closed my eyes and tightened my lips in what I hoped was a semblance of grief.

She leant across and touched my arm. "Please don't lose heart, Mrs Jones. I think that we may yet succeed."

"You do?" I looked up.

"It's borderline, but yes." She paused. "The reason I felt that I had to see you personally was to warn you that treatment might be a traumatic process – even more so than IVF – and to ask whether you and your husband are prepared for that. Am I right in thinking that you would have accepted AID had you not heard of microinjection?"

"I – I don't know. *I* would have accepted it, certainly, but Tom . . . well, he wants a child of his own so much."

"I understand that and, as I said, I think we have a good chance of succeeding."

I looked up. "You said that it might be more traumatic than IVF?"

"Yes." A silence. "You see, while there's every chance we can successfully fertilise your eggs with your husband's sperm, there's no guarantee that the resulting foetus would be . . . normal."

"But—"

"There never *is* a guarantee as such, of course. But there is a school of thought that suggests that if a man's sperm cannot fertilise an egg, there's a reason for it. Nature's way, in fact."

"But I thought you said that you'd had success with this technique?"

"Indeed I did, and we have, which is why I think we can be successful in this case. But you must understand that there are risks."

"I – I do understand that."

"But does your husband?"

"I think so. He told me he'd take almost any risk for the chance of his own child."

"Good. So long as you both do understand."

"Dr Kent, what exactly are the risks?"

"Firstly, that we don't succeed at all with the acute disappointment this would bring. Secondly, that you become pregnant but miscarry. Thirdly, that you have a child with a hereditary . . . weakness, or handicap of some kind."

"A serious handicap?"

"Possibly. Which brings me to the fourth risk – that the child, or children, could be either stillborn, or die in infancy."

I let out a sigh. "Put like that, it does sound risky, to say the least. But I know that Tom will want to try." I looked up again. "What are our chances of having a normal child?"

"I can't say." She studied me carefully, as though looking for something. "I've had to spell out the risks for you, Mrs Jones, but now I'm going to stick my neck out, and tell you that I think there's a very good chance. Greater than fifty per cent, although we may have to try more than once." She got to her feet. "I've taken up enough of your time now. You and your husband think about it and we'll discuss the practicalities of treatment if you decide to keep the appointment on Wednesday."

"Oh, we will, there's no doubt about that." I stood up myself and walked to the door with her. "Dr Kent, it's been very good of you to go to all this trouble."

"This is a special case, and I have every hope of a happy outcome."

"I – thank you. I'll see you down."

"Please don't trouble, Mrs Jones, I can find my own way out."

I watched till she was out of sight, then went back inside and fumbled for my cigarettes. I was shaking so much I couldn't get one out.

Nine

I'd managed to get a cigarette alight by the time the front door opened and Tom came in.

"Jo, you were brilliant." He sat down beside me. "Are you all right?"

"No," I said weakly. "I'd kill for a coffee, but I'm too shattered to make it myself."

"I'll do it." He vanished into the kitchen and returned a couple of minutes later holding two mugs. I thanked him, then said. "You were listening, then?"

"I told you we had the place wired. We've got it all on tape."

"Tom, I was terrified."

"Yes, and in all the right places, too."

"I mean it."

"I know." He put an arm round me, squeezed briefly. "You were still brilliant."

"You don't think she'll suspect anything?"

"I don't see how she can. Letting her stop you in the street was a master stroke."

"You saw that?"

He nodded. "From a safe distance. No, I don't think you put a foot wrong."

"You know what scared me most of all? When she asked for the bathroom – I wasn't sure whether there was any loo paper, and nobody would have a home without loo paper, would they?"

"We wouldn't have overlooked that."

"I know. It's just the way I was." I drank some coffee. "You said you've got it on tape. Where were you?"

He grinned. "In one of the downstairs flats. We'll take it back to Marcus in a minute."

"But what if she's still around? She'll see us."

He shook his head. "She isn't. She disappeared into the nearest tube station."

"How d'you know?"

"I followed her – at a safe distance. I'll tell you something," he continued. "Although Marcus was right to get you down here; having listened to her, I'm not convinced that her main purpose was to check our story."

"How d'you mean?"

But before he could answer, there was a knock on the door and he went to open it.

"Hello, Phil. Finished downstairs?"

"Yup. Just come to collect the bug."

I stood up as they came in.

"Jo, this is Phil, our telecommunications expert."

Phil was tall, gangly and about thirty.

"Hi." He grinned at me, then went over to the wedding photo, took something from behind it, and put it carefully into the bag he was carrying.

"How did you manage that?" I asked Tom, pointing at the picture.

"Computer imaging."

Phil was looking down at the biscuits on the table. "They goin' beggin'?"

"Help yourself," I said. "Would you like a coffee?"

"We haven't really got time," Tom said.

"It won't take a moment. Besides, we've got to clear all this up."

He shrugged and smiled. "All right."

We washed and tidied up, then Phil drove us back in his departmental van.

*   *   *

72

"No, it's not particularly professional behaviour," Professor Fulbourn was saying, "but I wouldn't have said that it was unethical in any way."

It was a little over an hour later and we were in his office at St Michael's. He'd been so interested when Marcus told him about Dr Kent's visit and the tape that he had asked if he could hear it for himself.

"Nor slanderous?" Marcus asked with a perfectly straight face.

Prof grinned. "Not even that. She's perfectly entitled to express her surprise at my methods. Eccentric, certainly, perhaps even obsessive – that's how I'd describe her on the basis of this."

At the word 'obsessive' I glanced at Tom, but he appeared not to have noticed.

"So everything she said was fair and truthful?" Marcus said.

"I wouldn't have put quite such an emphasis on the risks myself, but by and large, yes." He paused. "My overall impression is that, for whatever reason, she very much wants you as patients."

"That's also been my impression throughout," said Tom.

"Then why did she go out of her way to emphasise the risks the way she did?" I asked.

"Trying to cover herself?" Tom said. "Preparing us for some inevitable disappointment?"

"You might have something there," Prof said thoughtfully. "She *wants* to treat you, and yet it's as though she knows it isn't going to go smoothly."

Marcus said, "We come back to the purely financial motive. Perhaps she intends giving you one or two cycles of expensive failure before going for donor insemination, with or without your knowledge. She did make a point of telling you that you might have to try more than once, didn't she?"

"And she did ask me whether I'd been prepared to accept donor insemination before," I said.

"But the Murrells," said Tom. "We keep coming back to

73

them. It was their first cycle of treatment, remember? And yet Mrs Murrell heard them say that it wasn't going to be his baby."

"But we've only got Mr Murrell's word for that," said Prof. "And if it were donor insemination, I can't understand why they'd do a laparoscopy."

"Could it have been a GIFT procedure?" I suggested. "Putting sperm and egg together in her tubes."

"They'd only use that if there had been something wrong with her tubes, which there wasn't."

Tom said, "Professor, she referred to the semen you gave me as something of a challenge; then she went on to say she was surprised that you'd bothered with it. Was that semen capable of fertilising an egg?"

The Professor thought before replying. "Not very likely with IVF, no, so her surprise was in order. Perhaps that should have occurred to me when I was preparing it, but I gave you that sample specifically *because* it was a challenge, the kind of difficult case she's accepted in the past."

"What I'm getting at is this – is it possible, in your view, that she's genuinely intending to use it?"

"Yes, it is possible," he said carefully, "with microinjection."

"Is it likely?"

He took a breath. "To use her own expression, it's certainly a challenge. But until I've got more information, I can't really say, any more than I can say whether she's doing anything illegal."

"Hmm. Well, I think she's about as genuine as that sample you gave me."

"You've only heard her on tape, Tom," I said. "I was there. I could see her face, and the more I think about it, the more I'm convinced that she was being sincere."

"Oh, I'm sure she was," said Tom. "But sincere about what?"

Marcus turned to the Professor. "Did you find out whether there are any conferences being held today, Professor?"

"There is one, as it happens, but not a particularly interesting one. I certainly wouldn't have bothered coming up to London for it."

"So we still don't know whether she came up specifically to see you, Jo, or just took the opportunity while she was here."

We played the tape through again and talked round it to see if any more meaning could be teased from it, then gave up and left.

In the taxi, Marcus said. "Well, if nothing else, at least we know she's going to accept you as patients now, and that could be thanks to your efforts today, Jo." He paused briefly, then added, "If you hadn't pulled this off, I'd have thought seriously about cancelling the whole thing."

"But she did pull it off," Tom said.

"Yes, and it puts us ahead in the game."

After we'd dropped Marcus off (Tom said he'd accompany me to the station) I asked him if he and Marcus really did think of it as a game.

"No, that was just the rather old-fashioned way he has of putting things sometimes."

"The reason I asked is because I've been wondering whether we've got Dr Kent wrong."

"Never in a million years."

"Oh, she's obviously breaking the rules in some way, but the rules surrounding fertility treatment are so complex . . . what I'm saying is that she might be doing something that's theoretically unethical, but for the general good."

"The end justifies the means, you mean?"

"No, I mean something really quite small."

"For instance?"

"Oh, I don't know. But she does strike me as being just as passionate as Professor Fulbourn about helping childless women."

"So why was Mrs Murrell killed?"

"But was she? There's no proof, ReMLA said as much."

"It's too much of a coincidence. She was overheard telling

her husband about what *she'd* overheard, and then she was very quickly dispatched. Every instinct I have tells me she was murdered."

"By instinct, do you mean the fact that you and Dr Kent dislike each other?"

He smiled. "No more than the fact that she obviously likes you has influenced your opinion."

"Ha, ha. As I said at Professor Fulbourn's, I was impressed by her sincerity. Whatever it is she's doing, she believes in it."

"Jo, try to hang on to the fact that Mrs Murrell was murdered, murdered because something bad is going on there. Why all that security otherwise?"

By now, we were arriving at the station.

"Oh, you're probably right." I said.

But do I really think that? I wondered as the train pulled away. I'd agreed with him because I was exhausted, browbeaten. The only certainty I felt was that whatever it was Dr Kent was doing, unlike me, it wasn't for money.

Ten

"Nervous?"
    "Too right I am."
He didn't say anything to that, just kept driving. "It becomes real today. I've got to start taking the medicine and I don't know what it's going to do to me."

"Fulbourn'll be keeping a close eye on you."

"I feel as though I'm entering a tunnel," I continued as though he hadn't spoken, "there's light at the end of it, but it's a light I daren't reach. We're going to have to find our way out before then, and that's what makes entering the tunnel so frightening." Not to mention the fact that I have misgivings over the validity of what we're doing, I added silently.

He reached over and touched my hand. "It isn't going to happen, Jo. I'll be with you all the time to make sure it doesn't."

I gripped his hand a moment and tried to smile although it felt as though my lips were being stretched across my face.

We were high on Salisbury Plain, nearly there. The lowering grey sky seemed to be trying to push us into the grey-green earth; no skylarks today. And I couldn't even have a cigarette in case she smelt it.

"You'll feel better when we're in there face to face with her," Tom said.

"Like hell I will."

But he was right as usual; once Leila had ushered us into her presence, I knew I could cope.

"Well," she said, having greeted as and told us to sit down, "we now have the results of all our tests. These, broadly, confirm Professor Fulbourn's findings. You'll also be glad to know you haven't contracted any unpleasant infectious diseases since he saw you."

Her tone suggested an attempt at humour, so I dutifully smiled. Tom said, "Oh, good."

"So now we have to decide what treatment is appropriate. I expect" – this to Tom – "your wife has told you about my visit?"

"Yes. That's right," Tom replied in the tone of one who would like to say more but has been told not to.

"I took the opportunity to see her because the treatment I recommend will largely depend on attitude."

"My attitude, you mean?"

"Yours and Mrs Jones', yes. You've both already been through so much, and further unsuccessful treatment . . ." she tailed off and leant forward slightly. "You see, as I told your wife, you're a borderline case, Mr Jones. Yet I do believe, with patience and fortitude, there's a very good chance of a happy outcome. But I do have to be sure of your attitude. Do you understand what I'm saying?"

I leant over and gripped his hand. He glanced at me before replying.

"I think so, Dr Kent, yes. Like the Boy Scouts, we must be prepared, only in our case, for failure."

Dr Kent smiled. "I'm glad you can joke about it, Mr Jones. That's exactly the sort of attitude I mean. Oh, and the other thing is, you have both stopped smoking?"

"Yes," we lied in unison.

"Good. Now what I have in mind is this" – she looked at me – "your period is due to start in eight days, if I remember correctly, Mrs Jones?"

"Er – yes."

"Rather than wait a month, I propose to put you on what we call the fast track. We'll start you on Nafarelin today – that's a nasal spray very similar to the Buserelin Professor Fulbourn prescribed, so you'll be aware of the side effects?"

I smiled wryly. "Yes."

"This time, continue the Nafarelin, two doses per day, throughout the treatment. On day one of your period, you will commence daily injections of Humegon – preferably at St Michael's, so that they can also scan you at the same time. On day ten, you will come here and we will monitor the treatment for the final two or three days until your eggs are ready. Then we will give you a single dose of Pregnyl and collect the eggs thirty-five hours after that."

"So you want me to stay here, at the clinic, for two or three days before you take the eggs?"

"Yes. As I said earlier, you've both already been through a lot, so we want to monitor your hormone levels to make you don't shed your eggs before we can harvest them."

"That's fine . . ." I looked at Tom, "so long as my husband can stay with me. I do want him with me, if you don't mind."

"Far from it – we're geared up for couples here." She smiled, with her mouth, at Tom. "Besides which, we'll need you here, Mr Jones, to supply sperm before the eggs are collected, so it's as well to make sure you're on the spot."

Tom smiled faintly back. "Yes, indeed."

"After we've fertilised the eggs in the laboratory, by microinjection of your sperm, we'll want to study their development for at least three, possibly four, before replacing them in your womb, Mrs Jones."

"Oh," I said. "It was never more than two days with Professor Fulbourn."

"No. Microinjection is, by its very nature, a traumatic process, however careful we are. Look . . ." she rose, went over to her demonstration flip-charts and turned several of the sheets over, "the human egg. We have to pass a needle through the zona pellucida, here, into the cytoplasm, here, to deliver the sperm. Some of the eggs will not withstand this treatment and will simply disintegrate." She returned to her desk and sat down. "That's why I'm hoping to harvest at least ten eggs from you, Mrs Jones. We will microinject all of them, and if more than half develop into embryos, we shall have done very well. I hope to replace at least four embryos into your womb, but I must be certain that they all have a good chance of bringing about a pregnancy. That's why we need the extra time."

"And you want me staying here during that time?"

"Certainly. My past experience has shown that the more rested and relaxed the recipient, the better chance of a favourable outcome."

"And Tom will be able to stay with me throughout?" This was critical so far as I was concerned.

"Of course, so long as he helps you to relax." Tom gave me an encouraging smile, but Dr Kent went on. "Although I must sound a note of warning here. There must be no sexual activity. I'm sorry if this seems a hardship, but it's absolutely imperative."

"We understand," I said, glancing at Tom.

He nodded and murmured, "Yes."

"Good. Now, here are three weeks supply of Nafarelin, and a prescription for Humegon for you to give Professor Fulbourn."

She showed me how to use the Nafarelin (one measured spray per nostril twice a day).

"And you want me to start this immediately?" I said.

"When you get home, yes, and continue it through the Humegon treatment. It's really not much different from the Buserelin you used before." There was a short pause before she continued. "I think that's covered everything. Was there anything you wanted to ask me about?"

"There were a couple of things," Tom said.

"Yes?"

"We were hoping you'd show us the accommodation. And" – he smiled – "I must admit, as a salesman of medical equipment. I'd regard it as a real favour if you'd let me see your micromanipulator. Professional interest."

"Certainly I can show you one of the suites for patients, there is one empty at the moment. As for the laboratory equipment, well, it's not something we usually do, but . . ." she hesitated, regarding him, "Let me check whether it's in use at the moment." She glanced at her watch, then picked up the phone and keyed in a number. It occurred to me that both she and Tom were making an effort to be pleasant to each other.

"Carla? It's Davina. I have two patients with me at the moment who have expressed an interest in the micromanipulator, would it be possible . . . ? No, nothing like that, just a couple of minutes . . . fine, we'll be round."

She replaced the receiver and looked up. "She's just finishing off something, so if I show you the accommodation first, we should be just about right."

She led us back along the corridor to the main hall and up the stairs. Tom's eyes flicked briefly round, looking for the blind spot I guessed. Dr Kent ushered us through a door on the upper landing.

"This is what we call the patients' corridor. There are four self-contained suites, and a nurse is always on call in the room at the far end of the corridor."

She opened the door marked 4 and stood aside for us to go in. Inside the light, spacious room were two single beds. One was the sort of bed you'd expect to find in a hotel, the other was a hospital bed, although of a rather superior kind. The room was comfortably furnished with a dressing table, desk, TV and armchairs.

"Each suite has its own bathroom," she said, opening a door and showing us. If it hadn't been for the hospital bed, the room could have been in a good hotel. I said as much.

Dr Kent smiled. "As I said earlier, we feel it's very important for you to be in a relaxed atmosphere."

"Well, you've certainly achieved that."

"Thank you, Mrs Jones."

We descended the stairs again, then went back along what

I thought of as her corridor, past her room, the scanning room and round a corner. "Here is our theatre where we carry out egg collection, whether by ultrasound or laparoscopy." She opened the door so that we could see inside. It was small, but well equipped, with its own recovery room to one side. "It's next to the laboratory, so that the harvested eggs travel as short a distance as possible," she said.

"And that's where they're fertilised?" Tom asked.

"Yes, either by IVF or microinjection. Let's go and see whether Dr Goldberg is free yet."

She led us round another corner, past a door bearing the legend: LABORATORY. NO ADMITTANCE FOR UNAUTHORISED PERSONNEL. The corridor seemed to be parallel with the outside wall, and I guessed it ran round the whole of the inside of the building.

Dr Kent stopped at an open door, tapped and went in. A woman looked up from the desk where she had been working.

"Carla, These are the two patients I told you about. Mr and Mrs Jones. Mr Jones's firm markets medical equipment, which is why he'd like to see our micromanipulator." She turned back to us. "This is Dr Carla Goldberg, Scientific Director and my deputy."

Dr Goldberg stood up and came from behind her desk. "Good-morning," she said.

'Hi there' might have been more appropriate, since she was very clearly American, in appearance somehow, as well as accent. She was about my height, five feet four, with a slim, almost wiry body. Very dark hair in ringlets framed a small-featured, conventionally attractive face, made somehow plainer than it need have been by gold-rimmed spectacles.

"Does your firm manufacture micromanipulators, Mr Jones?"

"Not manufacture, no," Tom said with a smile, "but we are considering importing them."

"I see."

"Which is why I'm very keen to see your equipment."

"Well, there's nobody using it at the moment, so let's go."

We followed her through a door which led directly into the lab. This had been partitioned longways, and the side we were in was a conventional laboratory with shelves of reagents, a centrifuge, analysers, balances and dispensing equipment. Behind the glass partition, a black girl wearing a gown and face mask was taking a tray from an incubator. We went through another door into a smaller room.

"Well, there she is," Dr Goldberg said, indicating a stainless-steel microscope surrounded on all sides except the front by a Perspex cabinet.

Tom slowly approached it.

"Linear flow cabinet?" he asked, looking round at Dr Goldberg.

"That's right."

"Can you show us how it works?"

"Sure."

She seated herself in front of it and flicked a switch. An electric motor started up and a fluorescent light stuttered on. A breeze touched me as the fan pushed out the linear flow of sterile air which protected the eggs from infection.

"Here," Dr Goldberg indicated a delicate piece of equipment to her left, "is the low vacuum suction tip which picks up the egg and holds it in place. And over here is the glass pipette that injects the sperm." She indicated to her right.

"Beaudouin syringe?" Tom asked.

"A modified version, yes. Would you like to take a look?"

"Please."

She manoeuvred tip and pipette under the microscope and stood up. Tom took her place and looked down the eyepieces.

"Very nice," he said. "Beautiful." After a few moments, he looked round at Dr Goldberg. "Operating this must take a very high degree of technical skill."

"It certainly does," she said dryly. "Our technician. Chrystal, who's very good at it, gets paid almost as much as me."

Dr Kent said, "I mentioned to you earlier that the injection of the sperm is a traumatic process that can often actually destroy the egg; well, Chrystal has the best survival rate I've ever heard of. I can't think how we'd manage without her." She paused after this speech, then said, "If you've seen enough now, Mr Jones . . . ?"

"Of course. Thank you very much for showing me the equipment, Dr Goldberg."

"My pleasure."

We followed her back through the lab. I looked at the technician, Chrystal, with new interest; the work she was doing looked so mundane, yet I had the feeling Dr Kent hadn't exaggerated her worth.

Back in Dr Goldberg's room, Tom thanked her again somewhat fulsomely.

"You wouldn't have a spare brochure on the micromanipulator, would you? I'd be most grateful . . ."

"I'll have a look." The slightest edge of impatience had crept into her voice: she was tired of him and I couldn't altogether blame her.

She pulled open a drawer of her filing cabinet and shuffled through it a moment before extracting a glossy brochure and handing it to him.

"Is that the sort of thing?"

"It certainly is – may I keep it?"

"Sure—"

She broke off as the door opened and Chrystal came in.

"Carla, we need to order – oh, I'm sorry," she said as she saw us.

"That's all right Chrystal, we're just going," said Dr Kent quickly. "Er – this is Mr and Mrs Jones, new patients."

Chrystal really did say, "Hi there", for she, too, was an American.

Dr Kent led us back through the middle of the house to the main hall where we said our goodbyes.

"We'll look forward to seeing you both in just over a fortnight," she said, seeing us off the premises.

"I think we may have overstayed our welcome," I said as we drove away.

"I know damn well we did, but I had to see as much as possible to compare with the plans." He smiled. "I'm sure she'll put it down to my general pushiness."

"I hope so." I found a cigarette and lit it. "God, I needed this."

"She will," he repeated. "I'm going to have to get into Kent's office somehow, possibly Carla's as well. Cold fish, wasn't she, Carla."

"Probably in response to the warmth of your charm." I grinned at him to take any sting out of it.

"Funny how the scientific side of it is all-American. Not to mention Cal."

"Perhaps Carla and Chrystal knew each other before they came here."

"Yeah, I'll bet you're right." He glanced at me. "D'you still have doubts?"

"I honestly don't know, now." I drew on my cigarette. "The strange thing is, I found her, Dr Kent, a lot more believable at the flat. In the clinic, she's somehow more—"

"Clinical?"

"Yeah." I sighed and looked down at the package on my lap. "The thing I have the most doubts about is taking this stuff."

Eleven

I took my first dose of Nafarelin that night before bed and was pleasantly surprised to wake up the next morning without suffering any side effects, other than a slight headache – and so throughout the day at work. I arranged with Mrs Compton to be away as from the twelfth and for Mary to take over.

The full force of the side effects hit me the next day, Friday. I'd heard about hot flushes, but the half had not been told me. It was like a heated tidal wave coming from somewhere in my middle, flooding up through my body to my face.

"Are you all right?" Mary asked. "You've gone ever so red."

"I know. I'll go and sit down a few minutes. I'm sure it'll go off."

I went to my office and after a while, the tide receded.

The next few days were awful. Night sweats that left me drenched and drained the next day. More hot flushes, a nagging headache and a feeling of being bloated. And an increasing conviction that it was all for nothing, that I wouldn't be able to cope with it even if there was something going on at the clinic.

On the third day, Monday, I phoned Marcus and told him I wanted out. He said. "It's the drugs you're taking. Why don't you talk to Profess—"

"No. There's more to it than that, I—"

"Jo, talk to Professor Fulbourn, he'll be able to help you."

"No Marcus, I'm sorry, but I've made up my mind. And I'm sorry to have wasted so much of your time."

86

I put the phone down and was immediately overwhelmed by guilt, then almost tearfully grateful when the Professor phoned me five minutes later.

"The symptoms are almost certainly at their worst now," he said after I'd described them to him. "Give it just two more days. Trust me."

On his advice, I continued at work (brooding at home would only make me feel worse, he said), and by the end of the following day, I did feel slightly better. Or maybe I was just learning to cope.

I've a bloody good mind to tell Marcus I want *twenty* thousand, I thought.

On the sixth, a Thursday, I went to St Michael's to collect the ampoules of Humegon and have the first scan.

"Are you feeling any better now?" Prof asked. "You do sound a little better."

"A bit. Still pretty ropy."

He nodded. "I think it's possible the Humegon will ease the symptoms further, it often happens that way. Still, shall we have a look at how your ovaries are doing?"

He scanned me himself and I was surprised at how proficient he was. I suppose I'd thought anyone old enough to be a Professor would have lost the touch.

"All quiet here," he said. "I'll give you the first jab now, if you like."

He wielded the syringe as deftly as he had the scanner. I told him so.

He chuckled. "Thank you. I'm afraid you won't be saying that to whoever's doing it in a week's time, though."

"No, possibly not," I agreed feelingly.

He looked at me a moment before saying quietly, "Messrs Evans and Jones have been giving me a clearer idea of what you'll be up against. I think you're a very brave young lady."

I felt myself flush – again.

"Please don't," I said. "You'll have me in tears in a

minute." I meant it. He was a gentleman, even more than Marcus.

"There," he said gently. "Here's a week's supply of Humegon, and I'll see you again on the twelfth."

I took a taxi to Whitehall (they were paying the expenses) where I found Marcus, but no Tom.

"He's in Salisbury with Combes, the security firm," he told me.

"He's still not found a way of circumventing the system, then?"

"He may have," Marcus said cautiously. "That's why he's down there now, checking it out." He paused. "I'm sorry you've been feeling so low. Was Professor Fulbourn of any help?"

"Very much so, thanks." I told him how the symptoms might improve now I'd started the Humegon.

"I hope so," he said.

"So do I." My turn to pause. "Have there been any further developments?"

"Yes, as a matter of fact. We've found out a bit more of Dr Kent's previous history. She did all her medical training in Liverpool and was actually a consultant obstetrician there for a short period, before suddenly making a sideways move to the recently opened fertility clinic – this was back in the seventies."

"Why did she do that?"

"I don't know all the details, but apparently, she was something of a firebrand. Anyway, she was very successful in this new field until resigning under a cloud in 1986."

"Why?"

"Again. I don't know the whole story, but a woman she'd helped to become pregnant later killed her baby. After that, she went to America."

"Really? Did Tom tell you about the Americans at Catcott?"

"Yes, and that's not the only connection. We've done a bit of digging and discovered that Fertility Enterprises, who own the clinic, are themselves owned by Fertility Incorporated. They're a rather shadowy concern—"

"But American?"

"Exactly."

"Where does that leave us if we do find dirty business at the clinic?"

"I don't think it makes any difference so far as the British end is concerned. If they're breaking the law, then they're breaking it, whoever owns them. But I haven't told you the most curious thing yet."

"Well?"

"Dr Kent actually grew up in Catcott Manor – it was owned by her father. He sold it to National Heritage ten years ago, then leased it back from them and went on living there. He died about five years ago while Dr Kent was still in America. National Heritage wanted to buy the remaining five years back from her, but she refused and used some of the money her father had left her to have it converted for use as a clinic."

"Was it worth it, for just five years?"

"It must have been. I suppose."

"And there are only a few months left now?"

"Five, to be exact."

"As you say, its curious . . ."

I left to catch the train home before Tom came back. He phoned me that evening to say he was sorry he'd missed me and to ask how I was. I asked whether he'd had any luck with Combes and immediately sensed him clamming up.

"Don't know yet," he said. "It needs a bit more thinking about. I'm sure we will find a way."

I wasn't so sure I liked the sound of the 'we', although he might not have meant me. We talked a little more about the American involvement and Dr Kent's strange homecoming without really getting anywhere, exchanged a few pleasantries and rang off.

I don't know whether it was the Humegon, but I did feel

better as the week went on. I'd arranged for my GP's nurse to give me the injections, and good though she was, my backside grew increasingly tender, as Prof had predicted.

On the eleventh, I handed over to Mary, went home and packed before leaving for London and St Michael's the following morning.

Prof did the scan himself again.

"I can see ten follicles," he said, "maybe more. That's good. They certainly won't be able to complain about the response."

I asked him if he could tell me when the eggs were likely to be harvested.

"I couldn't say for sure at the moment," he replied. "Perhaps as long as a week, certainly no longer. I'll have a better idea when we've checked the hormone levels in your urine. We'll be needing two samples a day from you from now on."

I left them with the first in exchange for another Humegon injection. Some exchange! Already, the very sound of the word was enough to make me clench every muscle in my backside.

I went round to the flat, unpacked my night things, then phoned Marcus to tell him I'd arrived. He told me there were no further developments and to relax while I could.

Tom and Holly took me out that night to see the new production of *An Inspector Calls*, and somehow, Priestley's exposition of how we all depend on each other, need to be able to trust one other, reconciled me to the job we were doing.

The next day (between urine samples and Humegon) I managed to fit in both the Tate and the National. Professor Fulbourn told me my hormone levels were fine and that the eggs would probably be collected in five days.

In the evening, I had dinner with Marcus and his wife, Gillian, at their large house in the suburbs. It needed to be large, since they had four daughters, although two of them had left home.

"We're the reason Daddy's so bald." Kirsty, the youngest gravely informed me.

"*Kirsty!*"

"Sor-ry."

Her mother gave her an 'I'll deal with you later' look before turning back to me.

"I used to be a nurse myself before the brood came along."

"Really? Whereabouts?"

"Guy's."

"D'you miss it?"

"Mm, I do, sometimes."

"Would you want to go back?"

"I've thought about it. I do get the feeling, though, that I'd be hopelessly out of date."

"Not necessarily. Some aspects never change."

"For instance?"

We compared our respective periods with Marcus throwing in the odd observation, not an unpleasant way to spend an evening.

The following day was the last in London and we held a council of war at Whitehall.

"Has Professor Fulbourn been able to tell you yet when the eggs will be collected?" Marcus asked.

"He thinks the eighteenth. But whenever it is, we'll have thirty-five hours warning."

"Have you sorted the sperm out with the Professor yet?" Tom asked.

Marcus nodded. "As soon as we know when it's going to be needed, I'll warn him. Vince can collect it and bring it down."

"Who's Vince?" I asked.

"Our ton-up boy. Motorcyclist. We can arrange the actual hand-over when you contact me."

"That shouldn't be a problem," Tom said. "They may not want Jo moving about, but they can hardly object to me driving away for an hour."

"I want to be out no less than a day before the eggs are due to be replaced, so we'll need to find out what's going on before then. Have you worked out yet how you're going to bypass the security, Tom?"

"I think so. I'd rather not go into details until we're down there and I can check out whether or not it can be done."

"Does it need me?"

"Hopefully not."

"I hope not too, since on the second night, I'll probably have the injection of Pregnyl. Prof warned me that it might make me feel as bad as the Nafarelin did at first."

"So if you do need Jo," Marcus said to him, "you'd better do it the first night you're there."

"I'll make that decision when we get there."

I said to Marcus. "One thing that has been worrying me: what if we do get caught? I don't want to end up like Mrs Murrell."

"Tom'll be armed, and I'll be not far away, at the Pheasant Inn. The problem will be if they catch you before you've found anything and they sue us."

"Could they do that?"

"Not really, but it might mean them getting away with whatever it is they've been doing, which would be a shame."

There wasn't much else we could discuss or plan until we were actually there, and the meeting broke up shortly after this. I was on my way out when I remembered something.

"Did Catcott ever bill us, Marcus?"

"Yes, and it's been paid."

"Oh. You didn't say. When was this?"

"A few days after your last visit there."

"How much was it in the end?"

"Three thousand nine hundred pounds."

He'd probably already paid it when I'd told him I wanted out, I thought with a smile on my way downstairs. No wonder he'd got on to Prof so quickly.

What wasn't so amusing was the fact that it was the same amount as the Murrells had paid.

Doesn't mean anything, I told myself.

Tom and Marcus had both invited me to their homes for the evening, but I'd already decided to stay in the flat. I wanted to think things over by myself, and it was the last chance I'd have.

Think ten thousand pounds, Josephine, I kept telling myself as I travelled to St Michael's and then back to the flat. It didn't help me to sleep, though.

Twelve

"If you'd like to leave your cases here while you take your car round to the back to park," Leila said smilingly to Tom, "I'll show you up to your suite when you get back."

"OK."

"Did you have a good journey down?" Leila asked when me he'd gone.

"Fine, thank you."

"Do have a seat while you're waiting."

"Thanks."

She picked up her phone. "Dr Kent? Mr and Mrs Jones have arrived . . . yes, I'll tell her."

She replaced the receiver. "Dr Kent would like to see you before lunch, Mrs Jones. I'll take you along after I've shown you your room."

"Fine."

Tom came back in.

"Can I take one of the cases for you?" Leila asked him.

"Certainly not," he said indignantly, picking them both up.

She laughed. "I'm stronger than I look," she said. "But thanks anyway."

To my surprise, she led us away from the stairs and along Dr Kent's corridor. We went past her room, round the corner to the theatre, where Leila stopped and pressed a button in the wall opposite, and I realised that what looked like a recess was in fact the lift shaft.

"I didn't realise you had a lift here," Tom said.

"It's used mostly for patients coming in and out of theatre," Leila explained, "So normally, we do ask you to use the stairs."

There was a click as the lift arrived and Leila pulled the outer door open. It was big enough to take a supine patient; quite fast too, I could feel the weight on my feet as it rose. Leila opened the doors again after it had stopped.

"You're just here in number three," she said, producing a key and opening the door that stood opposite the lift. Tom carried the cases through, set them down and looked round.

"There should be everything you need," Leila said. "The *en suite* bathroom and toilet's in here, tea and coffee making facilities over here . . ."

We didn't tell her that Dr Kent had already shown us one of the suites.

". . . and here's what we call the panic button, beside your bed, Mrs Jones. You must push it if you feel unwell, or need attention. The on-call nurse at the end of the corridor will come straight away. She has a pass key."

"I take it I can press it if I think my wife's unwell?" Tom said.

"Of course you can." She paused briefly. "The other thing is security. Because of the nature of our work here, we do have quite an elaborate security system." She grinned. "You saw one of our security guards last time you were here, didn't you?"

"Caliban, you called him," Tom said.

"I shouldn't have really, Dr Kent doesn't like it. His real name's Calvin. You won't forget, will you?" she said anxiously.

"I don't think I'd dare," Tom said, smiling back at her.

"If you go downstairs at night, an alarm goes off in the security room, so it's best to try and avoid it. If you do have to go down for any reason, call the guard first, OK?" She indicated the telephone.

"OK. But why do you need such tight security?"

"Well, we do have a lot of valuable equipment here, but the

main reason, I'm afraid, is because of the extremist groups who don't approve of what we're doing."

"What extremist groups would that be?"

"I don't know all their names. The worst one's called Nature's Way, but some of the pro-life groups don't think much of us either."

"But that's ridiculous! Why ever not?"

Leila shrugged. "Because they think it's not natural, I suppose. You'd have to ask them."

Tom shook his head in disbelief and outrage, then said, "Can we use this phone to call outside?"

"You can ask reception for an outside line during the day, but it only goes through to security at night. I'll leave you to unpack now. If you'd like to come down in a minute, Mrs Jones, I'll take you to Dr Kent."

She smiled again, then left, gently pulling the door to behind her.

I sank into the nearest armchair. Tom hoisted his case on to his bed.

"Fancy a coffee?" he said.

"I'd better not keep Dr Kent waiting."

"It won't take long." He went over to the kettle, filled it and plugged it in. "Well, whatever's going on here," he said quietly. "I don't think Leila's any part of it."

"You're only saying that 'cos she's bubbly and sexy and bats her eyelids at you." I was still feeling bloated (I'd put on weight) and rather dowdy.

"Not at all. The others we've met are all constrained and defensive. She's just open."

"Hmm. Hurry up with the coffee while I use the loo."

When I came back in, he was examining the window.

"It's double glazed," he said, looking round at me. "I wonder why."

"Gets cold up here in the winter, I expect. Is this my coffee?"

After I'd swallowed it, I left him unpacking and went

downstairs to find Leila, who showed me through to Dr Kent.

After the usual greetings and enquiries, she asked me how I'd been feeling. Awful, I told her.

"I'm sorry to hear that – you should have phoned me."

"Professor Fulbourn's staff were very helpful." Better not tell her I'd had the sole attention of the great man himself.

"I'm sure they were." She paused. "Do you have their reports with you?"

"Oh, yes." I took them out of my bag and handed them to her.

"Good hormone levels, and at least ten follicles," she said after studying them a few moments. She looked up. "You did stop smoking, didn't you?"

"Oh yes, Dr Kent."

"Good girl. Well, shall we take a look at you now on the scanner?"

As before, she left me to undress. With a towel round my midriff, I raised myself onto the examination bed.

"I can see what Professor Fulbourn means," she said a few minutes later. She indicated my ovaries on the screen with the follicles round the edges. "I think there may be more than ten – a vaginal scan should tell us tomorrow."

"That picture, Dr Kent – I can't get over it. It's ten times better than the one at St Michael's."

"It should be. This is the Colour Flow Doppler system. It's from America, the very latest development."

"Well, it's very impressive. Can you say when you'll collect the eggs?"

"That's just what I'm wondering myself." She studied the screen again, moving the sensor slightly. "I think you're a day ahead of Professor Fulbourn's estimate, in which case, we'll give you the Pregnyl at midnight tonight and collect the eggs on Monday."

Tonight! She looked back at me and I tried to hide the panic on my face.

"We'll look at another urine sample and I'll decide when I see the lab result. But yes, I think it'll be tonight." She replaced the sensor, gently wiped the lubricant from my belly, then dropped the tissues into the bin. "Now, turn over and I'll give you today's Humegon injection."

Glad to hide my face, I did so while she prepared the syringe, holding it up to the light while she expelled the air.

"My God, they must have some butchers at St Michael's, your poor botty's quite blue."

"I thought it was in the nature of the thing," I said, panic jostling with acute distaste at her choice of wording.

"Not at all. Now, try to relax . . ."

She slapped one cheek and an instant later, sank the needle into the other. An old trick, but for all her fulsome expression, she did it very well and I hardly felt a thing.

"There," she said, "finished. Now, if you could get dressed and produce a urine sample for me, that'll be all for now. I'll tell you my decision as soon as I've seen the lab result."

Tom had finished unpacking and was staring out of the window when I got back to the suite.

"Any news?"

"They're probably going to give me the Pregnyl at midnight tonight."

"Tonight!" He crossed from the window and said quietly, "So they'll be taking the eggs from you . . . midday Monday?"

I nodded.

"Which cuts down on our time here. "He looked up. "And the Pregnyl could make you feel as bad as the Nafarelin did?"

"So the Professor said."

His mouth tightened. "In that case, we'll have to go snooping tonight."

"You can't! Not just after we've got here."

"Keep your voice down!" He nibbled at his lower lip. "Our just having got here doesn't make any difference, but I will need to take another look at the layout downstairs before . . ." He took out his packet of cheroots.

"Not in here," I said. "She was on at me about smoking again just now, and the smell of those things is so obvious."

He grunted and put them away.

"We can go for a drive after lunch," I said, "or a walk in the grounds, perhaps. I'm dying for a smoke as well."

"All right." He grinned nervily. "It's like being back at school, isn't it?" He looked at his watch. "Ten to one. We might as well go down for lunch now."

Leila showed us to the dining room, which was at the corner of the manor, so that the light came in from two sides. We were the first there.

"If you'd like to sit down," she said in her efficient, and increasingly irritating manner, "lunch will be served in just a few minutes."

"Is that a commonroom for guests through there?" Tom asked, indicating a connecting door. "Can we have a look?"

"Be my guests," she said, laughing at her own joke.

I followed Tom through. It was about twice the size of the dining room, also with two windows, but on the same side. There was a snooker table, an expensive-looking chess set and what looked like computer games, besides a well-stocked bookcase and several comfortable-looking armchairs.

"Obviously designed with the male uppermost in mind," I observed dryly.

"We're the one's with damn all to do."

"Not quite damn all," I murmured.

"Oh, the nifty fifty in the cubicle, you mean?"

"I do so love your powers of expression."

He gave me a quick grin before going over to one of the windows. These were lead latticed, with panels about six inches across. He looked out and down, then carefully studied the catches and frames, before moving to the other window and repeating the process.

"What are you doing?" I whispered as he came back over to

me. He put a finger to his lips and went to the door which led to the corridor. He opened it, glanced casually in each direction, then closed it again. He looked slowly round once more before returning to the dining room.

I followed him. It was still empty. He repeated his scrutiny of the windows and was gazing up at the ceiling when the door opened and a man and a woman came in.

"Mr and Mrs Jones, right?" said the man in a loud and hearty voice. He had an open, rather flabby face, thinning hair and a gut that was beginning to spill over his belt.

"That's right," Tom said.

"Boyton. Geoff and Denny, as in Denise. That's Denny, I'm Geoff." Denny smiled, with considerable effort. I thought. "Just got here, then?"

"An hour or so ago," Tom replied.

"We've been here three days. Denny had the final jab last night, which is why she's a bit below par. Let's sit down, shall we, er . . . I absolutely refuse to call you Mr Jones."

"Tom," said Tom.

"Jo," I said.

"As in Josephine, right?"

"That's right," I said, fighting down the beginnings of a strong dislike. We sat down at one of the larger tables.

"You a snooker man, Tom? My last snooker partner left yesterday."

"I have been known . . ."

I turned to Denny. "Are you really not feeling well?"

She smiled, rather wanly. "You know what it's like." She had long auburn hair and blue eyes and would have been pretty, but for the effect of the drugs.

"Yes, I do," I replied. "Why didn't you stay in your room?"

She glanced at her husband. "If it gets any worse. I will. The things we go through, eh?"

I smiled back at her. "I know. My turn soon."

Geoff was telling Tom he was a salesman for an engineering

company, and with a sudden perception, I realised that he was almost exactly the same type that Tom had modelled himself on, down to the macho defensiveness, which probably meant it was he who had the problem.

"When are you for the midnight stick-up?" Denny was asking me.

"Probably tonight," I said, laughing.

A girl came in with a tray of soup. It was pea, and very good.

"How long have you been trying?" Denny asked.

"Three years. How about you?"

"Five. Five," she said again, then abruptly put her spoon down and closed her eyes. A tear welled up and ran down the side of her nose. I glanced at Geoff, but he was still talking to Tom.

I put a hand on her shoulder. "Shall I take you up to your room."

"Yes, please," she said in a low voice. Then, more loudly, "Geoff, I'm going up to the suite."

"Oh. D'you want me to . . . ?"

"It's all right, Mrs Jones is coming with me."

"Oh, right. I'll be up later, then."

She composed her face as we went into the hall and started up the stairs.

"It's very good of you . . . after all, I hardly know you."

"Put it down to female solidarity." I said. "Which is your room?"

"Four."

Next to ours and directly opposite the door from the upper landing. As soon as we were inside, she sank on to her bed and started weeping again, this time holding nothing back.

"D'you want a nurse?" I asked.

"No."

I sat beside her, put an arm round her and said nothing, just let her cry it out.

After a while, the tears subsided and she wiped her eyes.

"I had no right to inflict that on you," she said shakily.

"You have every right. Why don't you tell me about it?"

"That would be a further affliction."

"So I'm a masochist."

She blinked and smiled. "You must be." She looked down at her hands on her lap. "It's very simple. We've been trying for a child for so long. Geoff . . ." she looked quickly up at me, "I'm not *blaming* him."

"It's the same for us," I said.

She gave a twisted, tearful smile. "Geoff must have sensed it. Anyway, six months ago, he was on the point of accepting donor insemination, when someone told him about this place. This is my second time here, and . . . I – I can't *bear* it." She swallowed. "You see, I actually became pregnant last time, and then, after ten weeks, I miscarried. I'd already had three cycles of IVF, and I can't take any more. But Geoff, he so wants a child of his own. He's not a secure person anyway, and this—"

"But it *would* be his own child, in all but biology . . ."

"I know it, and you know it, but we're still both here, aren't we?"

A key rattled in the door and, assuming it was Geoff, I stood up.

A nurse came in and came over to the bed.

"Mrs Boyton, your husband has just told me how you're feeling. Why didn't you come to me? That's what we're here for."

"Mrs Jones kindly helped me."

The nurse turned to me. "You should have brought her to me," she said, a reproving edge to her voice. "I'm sure you meant well, but it might have been something serious." She was about thirty, small, with a pretty, yet rather hard face. Her name badge said she was Jenni Lavington.

"Mrs Boyton just wanted a shoulder to cry on," I said.

"Even so . . ."

"There are times, nurse, when—" I stopped, aware I was overstepping my role.

Her lips tightened momentarily, but she didn't pursue it.

"All right, but you can leave her with me now." She turned back to Denny. "A nice cup of tea, Mrs Boyton?"

I moved to the door.

"Thank you, Jo," Denny called.

"Any time," I said, and left.

Geoff looked up as I rejoined them in the dining room.

"The nurse found you all right, then?"

"Yes."

"Denny's all right, is she?"

"She's fine now. It all got a bit much for her."

"I know how she feels," Geoff said.

I was saved from having to think of a reply to this by the waitress.

"Are you ready for your second course now, Mrs Jones?"

"Please."

It was salmon, oven baked with tarragon, served with the newest of new potatoes and an excellent salad. It was delicious. Just the thing to take your mind off the misery, the little restrictions, the oppressive watchfulness, the velvet strait-jacket that was Catcott Manor.

Thirteen

"What was the matter with Denny?" Tom asked. I told him.

Lunch was finished and Dr Kent had confirmed that I was to have the Pregnyl that night. Tom and I were walking in the walled garden behind the manor. The hedges, lawns and bushes weren't exactly immaculate, but they were quite well maintained and we could see someone working near the wall at the bottom. Tom had brought his binoculars with him.

"I'm feeling lousy enough as it is, now," I said. "If it was my fifth time, like poor Denny, I'd be feeling suicidal. That selfish boor, Geoff—"

"Yes, he is," Tom agreed, "but he does have a point of view."

"Like what?" I demanded, turning on him. I was still smarting from the injustice of Denny's plight.

By now, we were approaching the gardener. "All right if we go through?" Tom asked him, indicating the wrought-iron gate in the wall.

"Sure." He was in his thirties and rather tough-looking for a gardener, with pale-blue eyes and very short dark hair. "You can go as far as the wooden gate at the bottom, but don't go any further. Army land."

"Thanks," Tom said, opening the gate for me. The path leading from it joined the track which came round from the front of the manor and ran on through parkland studded with trees and bushes.

"Did you notice the bleep on his belt?" Tom murmured. "I'll

104

bet he's the other security guard, so watch what you're saying when he's around."

"All right, but what point does Geoff have?" I said again as soon as I was sure we were out of earshot.

Tom glanced quickly behind, then veered off the track behind a clump of rhododendron. A moment later, he had a cheroot in his mouth and was inhaling greedily.

"I needed that." He took another drag.

"Tom, what point—?"

"I gave up once, you know, but then it was just me I had to deal with. Being told I can't smoke by the likes of Kent – that's different."

"You were right, we are like a couple of school kids," I said. By this time I had a cigarette going myself. "And you still haven't answered my question – what point, or excuse, could Geoff possibly have for his treatment of Denny?"

"I've been thinking about it. I know that people say a child conceived by AID is no different from having one of your own, but I'll bet the people who say that the loudest are those who don't have to do it. I've just become a father, and my feelings before and after the birth were very different. I wouldn't be without Harry for the world now, but my feelings were very mixed before he was born. I just didn't think I was cut out for fatherhood. What I'd have felt like if I'd known it wasn't even my own child, I don't know."

"But that's just selfishness. What about your wife's feelings, her needs?"

"It's not that simple with AID. You're going to have to tell that child, or children at some time—"

"Why?"

"Because they'll find out for themselves if you don't. Blood groups, tissue types and so on. And then, when they're being difficult teenagers, they can say: 'You can't tell me what to do, you aren't even my real father.'"

"Tom, it isn't like that."

"I know it isn't, not necessarily, but if you're an insecure bloke like Geoff, that's what you'd be thinking. Your ego's already taken one bashing, and you're on the look out for others. It's no wonder he jumped at microinjection when he heard of it, and so will plenty of others. Like Marcus said, it's a gold mine."

"Is that what you think now?" I said slowly, "that this is simply about fleecing people with that particular problem? But as you said yourself, how does that explain the Murrells?"

"I don't know what's going on, Jo, yet. What I am saying is save your anger for whatever it is. Geoff's just another victim."

"All right," I said unwillingly, after lighting another cigarette. "He's still a selfish boor, though."

"I know. I had to listen to him while you were with Denny, remember?"

A distant report made us look round.

"Tanks," said Tom. "Over there, look." He pointed, then fumbled for his binoculars.

I could just make out something crawling like an insect across the horizon. Then, like us, it seemed to puff smoke, although it must have been ten seconds later that we heard the report.

"It's a Challenger," Tom said. "Two miles away."

"Isn't it dangerous, firing so close to the manor?"

"No, it's very strictly regulated." He dropped his cheroot and trod on it. "Let's see where this track goes, shall we?"

We followed it down through more rhododendron clumps until it ended at a wooden gate, presumably the one the gardener meant. The track was quite well used up to the gate, probably because of the heap of garden rubbish next to it, but fainter thereafter. A notice attached to it read:

DANGER. DO NOT PROCEED BEYOND THIS POINT.

"Probably some ancient right of way," Tom mused as we reached it. "It must be used occasionally or it wouldn't be visible at all by now." He leaned against the gate, then quickly drew back as it creaked rather alarmingly. "It's rotten right through. They probably can't agree on whose job it is to repair it."

More reports of gunfire reached us, louder now, but out of sight.

"Well, you can see why they double glazed the bedroom windows," Tom observed. "Or do I mean *hear* why?" He raised the binoculars again. "Good Lord!"

"What is it?"

"Look, over there." He handed me the binoculars and showed me how to adjust them.

Amid the scrub in the distance lay three derelict tanks — you could see they were derelict by the rust on their sides and their broken tracks. But they were in formation, their barrels held high, and they looked for all the world like ghostly sentinels saying, 'Abandon hope all ye who enter here.'

I shivered suddenly. "Can we go back, please, Tom?" I handed him the binoculars.

"All right." He took another quick look himself, then we turned and walked back up the track.

"They are a bit spooky, aren't they?" he said quietly.

"When are you going to contact Marcus?" I said after a pause. "You'll need to tell him about Monday. The sperm." I reminded him.

"Oh yes." He looked at his watch. "He should be at the Pheasant by now. I might as well drive over and see him."

"Shall I come?"

"Probably better not. Do what the doctor ordered — relax!"

"Ha ha."

The garden wall came into view, the stonework lit by the sun.

"Might as well go straight round to the car," Tom said.

"I'll come with you."

We followed the track up as it skirted the side of the wall

until it reached a garage and some sheds, besides which was the gravelled car park.

"Give Marcus my regards," I said as he got into the car. He shot me a frown which said, *Shut up.*

I smiled an apology and inwardly kicked myself. Could anyone have heard? Where was the gardener-cum-heavy?

Tom started the car, turned it and drove off. I waved, then made my way slowly round to the front of the manor.

Dr Kent was in the main hall, saying something to Leila. She looked up as I came in.

"Your husband deserted you for the afternoon, Mrs Jones?"

I thought quickly. "He's gone to look up an old friend in Devizes. I decided not to go with him." I made for the stairs as I spoke, not wanting her to get too close in case she smelt the tobacco smoke.

"Good. Relaxation, Mrs Jones. I can't emphasise it enough."

I smiled as I started up the stairs. She spoke to Leila again, but her eyes flicked back to me.

When I got to the patients' corridor, I knocked on Denny's door. After a pause it opened.

"Jo, hello," she said. She was wearing a bathrobe.

"Just wanted to see how you were."

"Better, thanks. I won't ask you in now as I've got the bath running."

"That's all right. I'm glad you're feeling better. You will come and talk to me if things get bad again, won't you?"

She promised she would and I went back to my own suite. I brushed my teeth in case I ran into Dr Kent again, then decided to have a bath myself.

I was lying on my bed reading an hour and a half later when Tom came back.

"Everything all right?" I asked, sitting up.

"Fine." He put a finger to his lips, went over to the radio and found Classic FM.

"You don't seriously think we're bugged, do you?" I said in a low voice as he came back over.

"I think it's extremely unlikely," he said quietly as he pulled up a chair beside me. "But you never know who might be passing outside. Besides, I rather like Classic FM."

"Sorry about what I said at the car, Tom." I told him what I'd told Dr Kent about him visiting an old friend.

"That should cover it all right," he said. "Marcus sends you his regards, by the way."

"Did you arrange about the sperm?"

He nodded. "Professor Fulbourn'll provide the sample for Vince at seven that morning – what's so damn funny?"

"Provide. You just said, provide. The thought of Professor Fulbourn having a – a nifty fifty. Sorry. It's this place, it's getting to me."

"It must be," Tom said, but then began laughing himself. "Vince'll need an hour and a half or so to get here with it, and I'll pick it up at about eight thirty."

"How? You can't just . . ."

"I'm a health freak, I go jogging every morning. I'll start tomorrow. On Monday, I jog up to the junction with the main road. Marcus'll be there and will give me the sperm."

"As long as you're not seen."

"I'll make sure I'm not."

"Did you arrange anything else?"

He hesitated. "Yes, as a matter of fact, I did."

I looked at him. "From the sound of your voice, I'm not going to like it."

"I'm going to try and get into Kent's office tonight, maybe the lab as well. The sooner we can find some hard evidence of what they're up to and get out of here, the better, wouldn't you agree?"

"Yes?" I was still suspicious.

"The thing is, I'll need your help."

"I *knew* it!"

"Keep your voice down," he hissed.

"All *right*. What help?"

"The security here makes it impossible to cover up any kind

109

of break in. I've been over it a hundred times, and the only way way is to make it look as though there's been a break in from outside, by some group like Natural Way, for instance."

I thought for a moment. "That's all very well, but what about Cal?"

"Exactly. He has to be immobilised."

"Immobilised? You mean overpower him and tie him up or something? I don't mean to be rude, Tom, but we've both seen him and—"

"I know. We're going to have to use this." He dragged out his suitcase from under his bed and fumbled in the hidden compartment. 'This' was an object like a pistol with a syringe on the top.

"A tranquilliser dart," he said.

"No," I said, shaking my head. "Definitely not. Nobody'll believe an extremist group could get hold of one of those."

"Don't you ever listen to the news? Extremist groups get hold of whatever they like these days."

"So what tranquillising drug are they supposed to have got hold of to go with that?"

"This." He took a phial from the compartment and handed it to me.

"Midazolam X," I read out. "Midazolam's supposed to be injected intravenously. Where were you intending to inject it?"

"In his bum, I suppose."

"Intramuscularly, in other words. That would take too long to knock him out."

"We've already thought of that. This stuff is a fast act-ing variant – thus the X. It also gives rise to a localised amnesia."

"What d'you mean, localised amnesia?"

"Well, he might remember the alarm buzzer going off in his office, but he won't remember the dart hitting him."

"Oh I see, so an alarm buzzer has to go off. So how are you going to bring that about?"

"We go to the top landing and use the blind spot to lower ourselves into the hall."

"I don't believe I'm hearing this."

"Then we go through the doorway under the stairs and along the passage to the commonroom. We remove the light bulbs, then I open a window. That'll trigger the alarm in his office and he'll come to investigate. You'll be waiting in the corner so that whichever door he uses, you'll be able to fire the dart into his—"

"*Me*? You want *me* to fire it? Absolutely not!"

"Keep your voice—"

"Tom, this has gone far enough."

"It has to be you, Jo. Those windows are heavy and you wouldn't be able to open any of them. And if I do it and he comes quickly. I wouldn't have time to get into position."

"But . . ." But the trouble was, I couldn't see any other way. "But what if I miss?" I said in a small voice.

"You won't," he said confidently. "You've seen him, nobody could miss a target that size. Besides, I'll have my gun."

"You bastard! You've had this planned all along, haven't you?"

I closed my eyes. The radio was playing the opening bars of Beethoven's Fifth.

Fourteen

Plop. The dart hit the pillow, an inch from the target. I was getting good.

I pulled back the spring mechanism, retrieved the dart and fitted it back into the gun.

Plop. An inch and a half this time. Still not bad. Tom was downstairs and I was in our room, a chair wedged under the door handle in case Nurse Jenni got nosy.

We'd gone for another smoke in the garden after he'd told me what he wanted me to do. I did all I could to dissuade him, begged him to think of another way, but it was no use, perhaps because I knew deep down there wasn't one. Tomorrow night was out because, if Denny was anything to go by, I'd be feeling pretty awful by then, and the night after that would be following egg collection, which was cutting things too fine.

Plop. Bullseye! Maybe there was hope yet . . .

Dinner was at seven and we were the last to arrive. Geoff and Denny were sharing a table with another couple. Denny gave me a smile as we passed them. Geoff was too busy talking to notice us.

Tom purposefully made for another couple, who were sitting at a table on their own.

"Mind if we join you?"

"Er – no. Of course not." They did, clearly, but Tom took no notice.

They were called Graham and Wendy Dacie. He was older than her and they both worked in a bank. Tom tried to pump them, but Graham wasn't having any. He smiled thin smiles, answered Tom's questions civilly enough and didn't give a thing away.

She was due to have her Pregnyl injection tomorrow night. I couldn't eat much, but then again, neither did she. I think it was some sort of casserole.

They say the waiting's the worst bit. Not necessarily true, but still pretty bad. After dinner, we walked in the grounds again, Tom going over the plan once more, presumably to put me at ease.

"Aha! Caught in the act!"

I let out a squeak as my cigarette described a smoky parabola. It was Geoff and Denny. Denny said, "Jo, shame on you! Didn't Dr Kent tell you it could reduce your chances?"

"It's only my second today, for God's sake!" I lied as I retrieved it. "I'm sorry, it's this place. It's been getting to me."

"I know exactly what you mean," said Geoff, even more inaccurately than usual. "Don't worry, we won't give you away."

"Thanks," said Tom. He drew on his cheroot. "Wouldn't like to have to face Dr Kent if she got really nasty."

Geoff laughed. "You and me both." He paused and turned, his face ruddy in the sunset. "Beautiful evening, isn't it?"

"Isn't it," we agreed.

By mutual accord, we walked slowly down to the gate and watched as the clouds bruised over and the bats came out. Denny put her arm through Geoff's; he smiled down at her and pulled her closer and I realised that for all their troubles, they loved each other. It made me feel a little envious, a little wistful, a little sad. It also calmed me.

Plop. We were back in our room.

"That's pretty good, Jo. I don't know what you're worried about."

"Bastard."

We watched TV and then pretended to read until midnight when another nurse (Sophi) came to give me the Pregnyl injection. It hurt.

Tom wanted the alarm to go in the security room at just after one, to give us as near an hour as possible before the general alarm went, so we waited while the old building slowly settled into silence.

We left at ten to one. We wore dark clothes over our night clothes and on our feet, appropriately, sneakers. Tom carried the equipment in a black haversack on his back. He left the door on the latch. The corridor was dimly lit.

We stole past number four, Geoff and Denny's room. A board creaked beneath my foot – I froze – Tom beckoned urgently from the landing door and the board squeaked again as I moved.

The upper landing. I heaved in a few breaths. Tom quickly checked below with his pencil torch, then lowered the rope and made it fast to the banister. He eased himself over and noiselessly descended hand over hand. A guarded flash from his torch told me it was my turn.

I swallowed, took another breath. Lifted a leg over. found a toe hold between the railings. Gripped the banister, swung the other leg – squeak of rubber sole on paint – grasped the rope and cast off.

My toe bumped against panelling with a hollow knock, then Tom's hands were guiding my feet to the floor. He gently propelled me through the doorway into the passage, then pulled the cord which released the rope, and a moment later, it was back in his bag.

Along the passage to the commonroom. We kept to the sides where Tom said the boards were less likely to make a noise. The muted mutter of a television came from the security room.

The commonroom. Tom eased the door open and we were inside. He looked at his watch and showed me – it was still a couple of minutes to one. Then he flicked the pencil beam round the room before lowering the black bag to the floor. He beckoned me over, put his arms round my thighs and lifted me so I could take out the light bulbs.

Then he opened the black bag. First came the dart gun, which he handed to me. Then, two stocking masks. He pulled his own on. I filled the syringe and fitted it to the gun first – hands remarkably steady – then pulled on my own mask. It hardly affected my vision.

Tom put his mouth close to my ear. "Ready?"

I nodded. He guided me gently into the corner of the room, then went over to the window he'd selected.

He checked his watch again, then slipped the catch and pulled upwards on the two small handles at the bottom. The window gave one muted squeal, then moved smoothly up. Tom ducked out of sight behind a chair. I felt cool air. My heartbeat was starving my lungs and I sucked some of the cold air into them.

Silence. Another deep breath. My hands were shaking badly now. I couldn't do it.

There was the faintest creak, and I could make out the door from the dining room opening. A click from the light switch, a pause, then a powerful torch beam sprang out, sweeping round the room until it fastened on to the open window. The door opened further and Cal's huge bulk moved inside the room as he flicked the torch beam round again.

He was about six feet from me . . . it had to be now. I raised the gun with both hands to stop the shaking, aimed at his buttock and squeezed.

Plop.

He gave a grunt and the torch went out as he dropped to the floor. I heard him scrabbling for the dart, he gave another grunt as he pulled it out. Then he came up to a crouch and the torch beam came on again, searching, finding and blinding me.

"I can see you, stand up."

Still blinded, aware only of his bulk lungeing at me, I tried to dart round an armchair but he reached over it and snatched

my wrist and pulled me to him. I fought down the urge to yell
as he yanked off my stocking mask. Then the torch beam slid
away as his knees buckled. Tom caught him and lowered him
gently to the floor.

I knelt beside him and felt for his pulse. I still couldn't see
anything.

"Are you all right?" Tom whispered.

I nodded. "Yes."

"What about him?"

"He's fine."

"We'll wait a couple of minutes for your eyes to adjust and
make sure no one's heard anything."

Silence. Shapes materialised as my vision came back. Tom
took off his sneakers and put on a pair of shoes from the
bag.

"Keep your ears open." He went over to the window and
the next moment, he was outside, pulling it closed.

I heard rather than saw him scratching at one of the panes
with a glasscutter, then he covered the glass with masking tape
and a second later, there was a pop and his gloved fist came
through.

The window was raised again and Tom climbed back inside,
making sure his feet rubbed against the window frame. He
changed back into his sneakers, and we quickly replaced the
light bulbs.

"We've got about fifty minutes," he breathed. "The lab door
first, then Kent's office, then Carla's."

"What about the dartgun?"

"Bring it."

We found it, packed it away in the bag and made our way
round to the lab. Tom took out a spray can and used it to
write on the wall next to the door: Leave conception to God
and Nature.

Then he took out a screwdriver, put it into the lock and
twisted it, marking the metal round the keyhole. We went to
Dr Kent's office.

One of his 'keys' soon had the door open. I carefully closed it behind us as he went over to the fire safe. A moment later, that was open too.

On the top shelf were folders containing insurance policies, work permits and contract forms. On the bottom were three loose-leaf ledgers. He took them out. They were headed: Stimulated DNA 1989–91, Replaced DNA 1990–93 and Nuclear DNA 1992—.

"Hold the torch a minute," he whispered, handing it to me.

All three of the ledgers contained case notes of couples arranged in alphabetical order. He opened the last, Nuclear DNA 1992 – turned some pages and pointed. The name Murrell leapt out at me. He turned to the end of the file. There, in Dr Kent's neat handwriting, was a single word: terminated.

He turned the pages back, pointed again and I froze.

Jones.

There wasn't much in our file, only ultrasound results and hormone levels, and if I had my way, there wouldn't be much more added to it.

Tom looked at his watch and showed me. One twenty. He pointed to the desk.

I carefully closed the curtains and he switched on the desk lamp, arranging the ledger beneath it. Then he took out a small camera. I turned the pages while he photographed them. There was something over twenty cases.

"What about the others?" I whispered when he'd finished.

He looked at his watch again, compressed his lips.

"All right," he said. "But we'll have to hurry."

When we'd finished we replaced the ledgers and closed the safe. In the corridor, he relocked the door and glanced at his watch yet again.

"We'll have to be quicker in Carla's room," he whispered.

I nodded and we started down the corridor.

Behind us, in the hall, the alarm screamed out.

Fifteen

W e looked at each other for less than a second . . .
"The lift," Tom said.

We sprinted, swerving round the bend in the corridor and Tom stabbed at the call button. There was a clunk. He pulled the door open and hustled me inside. His thumb found the button.

"Don't go across the corridor till I say, right?"

The lift rose. The alarm howled. The lift slowed, stopped. Tom eased open the doors, listening for a moment before going down on his knees and cautiously peering out.

"Go!"

I shot across into our suite and heard Tom close the lift door before following me.

"Quick, out of those clothes and into bed."

He stripped off his own clothes, pushing them and the black bag under his bed before pulling a dressing gown over his pyjamas and sliding his feet into slippers.

Voices sounded in the corridor. I realised the alarm had stopped. Tom went to the door, opened it and stepped out.

"What's going on?" His voice sounded strange after hearing him whisper for so long.

"It's the burglar alarm." said Nurse Sophi.

"It's stopped." said Geoff's voice. "D'you think we should . . . ? Dr Kent!"

"Has anyone been down?" said Dr Kent's voice.

"No. Have you called the police?" asked Geoff.

"Not yet, it might be a false alarm."

"D'you want us to come down with you, Dr Kent?" Tom.

"Please. Would you check the other patients, please nurse."

I heard floorboards squeak and the landing door open, then there was a gentle knock on our door.

"Mrs Jones . . . ?"

"Just coming . . ." I switched on the bedside light. A black sleeve was protruding from beneath Tom's bed. I pushed it under, then opened the door.

"Are you all right, Mrs Jones?"

"I'm fine. Where's my husband?"

"He's gone downstairs with Dr Kent."

"Have you called the police?"

"I expect Dr Kent's doing that now. If you'll excuse me, I must check the other patients."

"Of course." And check them in more than one way, I thought grimly. I closed the door and let out a breath. Tom's going down with Dr Kent was masterly, but it had been a very close thing. I began shivering as reaction caught up with me – we could have been seen coming out of the lift so easily.

What would they do now? Would they call the police? They'd have to. What would Dr Kent's reaction be?

I was shivering so violently by now that I crawled back into bed. It got worse. I got up again and went to the bathroom. Bolted the door, switched on the extractor fan and had a cigarette. Why hadn't we thought of this before? I wondered, watching the smoke spiral into the grill. I smoked another, brushed my teeth and went back to bed. I didn't hear Tom coming back because I was asleep.

I awoke the next morning to the sound of Classic FM, and looked at my bedside clock – half past seven. I had the same nagging headache and overall grunge feeling I'd had after starting the Nafarelin.

Tom came out of the bathroom, put his finger to his lips and came over. He was dressed in running shorts and sweatshirt.

"What happened?" I whispered.

"When the alarm went off, or when I went down with Dr Kent?"

"Both." I'd forgotten about the alarm going off when it shouldn't.

"Cal had set the security clock half an hour fast – I noticed when we looked in his office. Anyway, we then looked around until we found him and the broken window in the commonroom. She checked Cal over pretty thoroughly, then phoned the police."

"Did they come?"

He nodded. "I gave them a brief statement, but they'll want to see me again today. Both of us, probably. Kent insisted they didn't question anyone else last night."

"Does she suspect anything?"

He shrugged. "Not that I could see. She was absolutely bloody livid – couldn't wait to get to her office. I think the graffiti and the marks on the lab door put her mind at rest, though."

"Will she carry on as normal?"

"She told us she would. I'd better get on with my jog now."

"You're not serious, not after last night?"

"I'm a health freak, remember? Besides, I want to get the film to Marcus."

I open my mouth to say something, but he put his fingers over it.

"You get dressed and make yourself beautiful for breakfast."

"Oh, bog off, you patronising bastard."

Which he did.

How was he going to get the film to Marcus, I wondered. And why was he on such a high? Then I remembered how near risks had seemed to do this to him before. But not me, I thought, I don't want any more.

I had a shower, then dressed slowly, glad to be able to do so without him being present. I wasn't worried on my own account – my libido was at minus something – I just didn't want him there while I was feeling so cankerous.

He arrived back, puffing and somewhat red of face, just as I finished.

"That was quick." The radio was still on, so I continued in a low voice. "Did you give the film to Marcus?"

"There wasn't time for that. I found a phonebox, called him and left it where he could find it."

"Wasn't that a bit risky?"

He shook his head. "There was no one about."

I sniffed at him and said, "You'd better have a shower before we go down. I shan't go with you if you don't."

He grinned and saluted – "I hear and obey" – grabbed some clothes and went into the bathroom.

We were the first down. We helped ourselves to cereal and found a table. I wasn't very hungry. Wendy and Graham Dacie came in next. Wendy said, "Good-morning," and Graham rather pointedly chose a table by themselves. Then Geoff came in and sat with us.

"How's Denny?" I asked.

"Not bad, considering." He lowered his voice. "They're collecting the eggs today, so she's waiting for the pre-med."

"Why a pre-med?"

"Oh, they're doing a laparoscopy again."

"Why?"

"I'm not sure. Something to do with the position of the eggs, I think." He turned to Tom, changing the subject. "Has anything more been said about last—"

He was interrupted by the arrival of the fourth couple who were staying and whose names I didn't know yet. They were closely followed by Dr Kent.

She waited for silence, then said, "Ladies and gentlemen, I'm sorry to interrupt your breakfasts, but I want to apologise to you for the disgraceful disturbance to which you were subjected last night. This was perpetrated by a protest group who object to the nature of our work here. I have no intention of allowing them to disrupt the treatment you are having, and I hope you feel the same. If we allow them to do this, they'll have won."

"Hear, hear," said Geoff.

She continued, "I'm afraid the police will be here asking you questions later this morning. Please bear with them, they're only doing their job. Leila will tell you when they want to speak to you. Once again, I apologise and hope it won't spoil your stay here." She looked round at us all, then made a dignified exit.

After a short silence, Tom said, "Makes you feel sorry for all the bad things you've said about her, doesn't it?"

"Yeah," agreed Geoff. Then, "What bad things?"

"Tom's speaking for himself," I said.

"Joking," said Tom.

"Oh," said Geoff. "Dunno what the police think they're gonna get out of talking to everyone. We were the only ones who saw anything."

"Routine, I expect. And they did warn us they'd want to speak to us again, in case we remembered anything else."

"True," Geoff agreed. "The funny thing is, I wasn't sleeping all that well last night, and I do remember a board creaking not long before the alarm went off. D'you think I should mention it?"

"Can't do any harm," Tom said casually. "Although it would probably mean the police staying here for longer, checking it out."

"Hmm."

"How sure are you? Old houses do tend to make noises in the night."

"Put like that, I'm not so sure."

"Don't let me influence you. Think about it."

I'd been looking down at my cereal bowl, afraid to meet Geoff's eyes. I looked at my watch and started.

"Tom, it's ten to nine and I'm supposed to be seeing Dr Kent at nine. I'll have to go – excuse me, Geoff."

"Sure."

"Regards to Denny."

I left the room and walked quickly up the stairs. I remembered the board creaking and hoped Tom had put him off saying anything. I brushed my teeth, tidied my hair and went down again.

Leila gave me her practised smile. "Dr Kent's ready for you now, Mrs Jones."

"Thank you."

Dr Kent called me in and sat me down.

"How are you feeling this morning, Mrs Jones?"

"Pretty rough. Much the same way I felt after starting the Nafarelin."

"Only to be expected, I'm afraid. Although at least you can see the light at the end of the tunnel now."

Funny she should use that expression, I thought, recalling how I'd used it myself on the way here.

She placed her hands on her desk. "Still, shall we take a look at how you're doing?"

I went to the scanning room, undressed and hoisted myself on to the examining bed. This time, as she had indicated yesterday, the examination was much more thorough.

"Aha, I thought there might be more eggs . . . there, you see them?"

I moved my head slightly to see past my outstretched thigh – she was indicating a point on the monitor. "I – I think so." Actually, I wasn't sure I could see anything.

"I know so. Keep still while I see if there are any more."

After further manoeuvring, she said she could see two others, then it was over.

"Come back into the office when you're ready, please," she said, and left me. I dressed quickly and went back through.

"I'm sure you have at least thirteen eggs," she said once I was seated. "And it will increase our chances if we can collect them all. However, to do this, because of the position they are in, it means we will have to perform a laparoscopy.

However, that shouldn't . . . Is there something wrong, Mrs Jones?" She'd seen the dismay in my face.

"No . . . that is, I was expecting it to be done by ultrasound."

"And so we would, normally, but in this case, laparoscopy is definitely indicated . . . yes?"

I stopped myself saying: Is Mrs Boyton also an exception? and said rather lamely instead. "I hate operations. I hated the last laparoscopy I had."

"I can understand that," she said gently, "but surely, Mrs Jones, you want to maximise the chances of success?"

"Of course I do."

"Microinjection is a traumatic procedure and it is important to have as many eggs as possible."

"I understand."

She smiled. "We'll make sure we're especially gentle with you. There really is nothing to worry about."

I smiled weakly, trying not to think of Mrs Murrell. "I'm sure you're right."

"Relax as much as you can today, and we'll see you tomorrow. I think perhaps you'd better have some sedative tablets."

"No thank – Perhaps I will." I said, not wanting to make any more waves than I already had. She went to her cabinet and counted some out.

"Thank you," I said. "I'll take one as soon as I get to my room."

Tom was still in the dining room, talking to Geoff. They were the only ones there. I was about to call Tom when a thought occurred to me and I walked over.

"Geoff," I said, "sorry to interrupt, but you did say earlier that Denny was having a laparoscopy today, didn't you?"

"That's right. Something to do with the position of the eggs. Wh—"

"Did she have one last time you were here?"

"Yes, she did, actually." He lowered his voice. "Is something wrong?"

I summoned a smile. "No. You've explained it to me now. It's just that I've got to have a laparoscopy as well. Not a problem."

"Oh, right. Good."

"I think I'll go up. Leave you two to it."

"I'll come up with you. I want to see how Denny's doing."

"In that case, I'd better come too," Tom said. "Make sure you two don't get up to anything you shouldn't."

My, we are the cheery cheeky chappie this morning, I thought sourly.

We turned on the radio again – this time it was some soprano trying for top C.

"Is it a problem?" he asked when I told him about the laparoscopy.

"Would *you* like to be unconscious on an operating table with Dr Kent holding a scalpel over you?"

"No I wouldn't, now you come to mention it." He paused, looking up at me. "But there's not a lot we can do about it, is there? Not without raising her suspicions."

"Tom, I don't like it."

"I don't blame you. Let me think a minute." He walked over to the window, looked out. The lady on the radio, thankfully, ceased her attempts. Tom turned and said, "Marcus is getting the photographs over to Fulbourn as soon as they're ready – I'll make sure he knows about this as well."

"How will that help?"

"Fulbourn might be able to work out what's going on today. Meanwhile, we'll keep a sharp eye on Denny. She should be conscious by this evening, shouldn't she?"

"Before then, but—"

"And if you *do* have to go through with it yourself, I'll make sure I'm conspicuously around for every minute you're in that theatre. The second I smell anything bad, I'll be in there."

"Tom, I'm frightened . . ."

His eyes met mine. "D'you want to call it off?"

Yes! "I – I don't know."

He put his arms round me, holding me close. "Nobody would blame you."

"But I wouldn't be—"

"Listen." He held my shoulders and looked into my face again. "There's a chance the photos we took may be enough for Fulbourn to work out what's going on. In which case . . ."

"But we wouldn't know in time."

"We might. I'll go and contact Marcus now and—"

The phone in our room rang and he picked it up.

"Oh yes, Leila . . . thanks. The police," he said to me, putting the receiver down. "They'd like a word with us. Come on, it shouldn't take long and they'd smell a skunk if we tried to put it off now."

Marvelling anew at his powers of expression, I followed him down.

Sixteen

The police had commandeered the dining room. There were two of them sitting at one of the tables, one in plain clothes, the other in uniform holding a notebook.

"Please sit down," the plain-clothes man said, indicating chairs in front of them. "I'm Inspector Wylye and this is Constable Bratton. Mr and Mrs Jones, isn't it?" He had a slight accent which I took to be Wiltshire.

"Yes," we both said.

"I know you gave us a brief statement last night, Mr Jones, but I hope you'll bear with me if we go over it again." He looked down at his notes. "You awoke last night at about one thirty?"

"That's right, I heard the alarm going off."

"Did you hear it, Mrs Jones?"

"Er – yes. It woke me up as well."

He turned back to Tom. "Are you sure you weren't awake before that, Mr Jones?"

"Quite sure, yes."

"What did you do then?"

"Put on a dressing gown and slippers and went to see what was going on."

"And?"

"Mr Boyton was outside, together with the on-call nurse. We were wondering what to do when Dr Kent arrived."

"What happened then?"

"Geoff – Mr Boyton – and I volunteered to go downstairs with her."

"Was the alarm still going at this stage, do you remember?"

"I . . . don't believe it was."

"So you and Mr Boyton went downstairs with Dr Kent. That would be the main staircase to the hall?"

"That's right. Dr Kent flashed her torch around, but we couldn't see or hear anyone. Then we went to the security office, which was empty."

"Which it shouldn't have been?"

"Not according to Dr Kent, no. We looked round, starting here, in the dining room. In the commonroom, next door, we found the security guard, lying unconscious, and a window open. Dr Kent checked him over, then went to her office to phone for the police. Geoff and I looked round, but all we could find was some writing on the wall by the laboratory. We showed it to Dr Kent and the police arrived quite soon after that."

"OK, that gives me quite a clear picture. Mr Jones, think hard . . . the alarm had stopped and you were going downstairs. Did you hear any noises from outside, voices, footsteps, a car door or engine?"

"I don't think so."

"You don't think so?"

"It's difficult to say. We were listening for noises inside."

"What about in the commonroom, when you were near the open window?"

"I can't remember anything."

"You see, Mr Jones, if it was the alarm that scared the intruders, they wouldn't have had much time to get away. You should have heard a car engine, or something."

"I can only repeat that I can't remember hearing anything."

The inspector didn't say anything, just studied him carefully, and after a moment Tom continued, "I suppose our minds were on what we'd found – the security guard." He stopped abruptly, then went on, "Can't *he* tell you what happened, Inspector? He's conscious now, isn't he?"

"He is, yes, but it seems that he can't remember much either."

"Concussion, I suppose. But he should remember when that wears—"

"What made you say concussion, Mr Jones?"

Tom shrugged. "Sorry. I assumed he'd been hit on the head."

The Inspector looked at him a moment as though deciding what to say next.

"As it happens, he'd been injected with a drug, which suggests to us that the . . . perpetrators knew all about the security here and came prepared."

"I hadn't realised that. Does it make a difference?"

"We don't know, yet." He looked at him a little longer before turning to me.

"Mrs Jones, I believe you said just now that you were also woken by the alarm?"

"Yes, I did."

"Are you sure you weren't awake before that?"

"As sure as I can be."

"Please think carefully. Did you hear anything else? Anything."

I pursed my lips and turned my eyes away for a few moments.

"I'm as sure as I can be that I didn't. But all the upstairs windows are double glazed, and very little noise from outside can get in."

"I was thinking of noises from the inside."

"I'm quite certain I didn't hear anything until the alarm went off." It was at this point that my body decided to let me down and I felt a hot flush flooding up through my face.

"You've gone very red, Mrs Jones – are you all right?"

"I was injected with a drug called Pregnyl last night, it's part of the treatment here. Flushes like this are one of the side effects."

"But it didn't prevent you from sleeping soundly?"

"No, the symptoms have only really hit me this morning."

"Inspector," said Tom, "it's unlikely that either of us would have heard anyone either getting in or creeping about downstairs last night, even if we had been awake. Why do you keep pressing this point?"

"Because we have to make sure that nobody inside was involved."

So Geoff had talked after all, I thought. Under this kind of pressure, I wasn't really surprised.

Tom said slowly. "But Dr Kent told us this morning that a protest group was responsible. And I must say I saw the broken window and the graffiti myself last night."

Wylye hesitated before replying. "There are one or two aspects which don't quite add up, sir. And as I said before, I am surprised, in view of how quickly you responded to the alarm, that no one heard the sound of their getaway."

Leave it, Tom, I thought. He must have received the message because he said, "Well, I'm afraid we can't help you, Inspector. And since my wife's not feeling well, I'd like to take her up to our room now, if you don't mind."

"Of course, sir. Although we may need to talk to you again later."

We didn't speak until we were in our room, then I said, "They know, don't they?"

"Not at all. All they've got is Geoff hearing a board squeak and the fact that no one heard a car leaving. They're just checking all the possibilities, that's all."

"But he said he wanted to talk to you again – what if he arrests us?"

"In that very unlikely event we tell them the truth. But Jo" – he took my shoulders – "it isn't going to happen. Try and stop worrying. I'd better go and try to contact Marcus now."

There was the faintest touch of impatience in his voice, so I didn't say any more. I thought it through, after he'd gone. Try not to worry, he'd said. I hated playing the vapouring female to his strong, steady male, but he wasn't the one who had to be pumped full of drugs, rendered unconscious and sliced open by Dr Kent.

Think ten thousand pounds Jo, I told myself, but the words that kept coming back were: Is it worth it?

I was feeling really rough, so I lay down on the bed and tried to think about life after Catcott. Strangely, I didn't want a smoke.

After a while, I got up and switched on the TV, something I never do at home, not during the day. The choice was between fatuous current affairs (affaires might have been more interesting) or gormless chat show. I turned it off and put on the radio, still tuned to the omnipresent Classic FM. It was playing a piece of music so restful that I lay down again. I couldn't name it, although for some reason, it made me think of horses.

Tom came in just as it was finishing.

"Shut up!" I said fiercely as he started to say something. The music ended and we were informed it was Beethoven's Sixth. Of course, 'Fantasia'! It must have been Beethoven week.

"Permission to speak?" Tom said.

"Sorry, just wanted to know what the music was."

"Oh. Well, I got through to Marcus and he'll have the photographs taken over to Fulbourn this afternoon. Hopefully, he'll contact us this evening."

"What, here?"

"I did check whether the occasional business call was in order."

Lunch. The police had gone. Geoff told us that Denny was still in theatre. After he'd gone back upstairs, Tom challenged me to a game of chess in the commonroom. He beat me easily, and his smug expression made me mad.

"Another?" I said.

"All right."

This time, I attacked immediately with all my major pieces and after a bloody slogging match, cornered him.

"Best of three?" he said grimly.

"No." The door opened. "Here's Geoff. Take it out on him. Any news yet, Geoff?" I asked him as I passed.

"Er – not yet, no."

I went back up to the suite and tried to do a relaxing technique, emptying my mind of everything but the feel of my limbs sinking into the bed. It was just beginning to work when Tom came in.

"Denny's out of theatre and coming round."

"Oh, good."

We went down and walked in the grounds. There was a smell of mown grass and birdsong. This time, I did want a cigarette.

"Rather a long time wasn't it, for a laparoscopy?"

"A hell of a long time," I said slowly. "Why, I wonder?"

"Perhaps Geoff'll be able to tell us at dinner time."

"Dinner time!" I exploded, surprising even myself. "This place is worse than a bloody prison."

"Oh? I didn't know you'd done any porridge. What were you in for?"

"Ha bloody ha. I feel like I've been here weeks. It's all right for you, you can go swanning off whenever you feel like it."

"So can you, Jo," he said quietly. "I knew a bloke once who was in prison, wrongly. Believe me, it's different."

I closed my eyes. "Sorry."

He put his arm round me. "No, I'm sorry, Jo. I know it's bloody for you. Please try to hang on."

At dinner, Geoff told us that Denny was fine and that the op had taken a long time because they wanted to make sure they got all the eggs. Hmm.

Marcus phoned just before eight thirty. Tom took the call, said, 'Yes', or 'I understand', occasionally before ringing off. He turned up the sound of the TV again before speaking quietly to me.

"Professor Fulbourn's looked over the data and made some preliminary comments. Of all the cases we photographed, only the last nine had laparoscopies, and of these, Mrs Murrell was the only case terminated. They've checked five of the others and they're all alive and well, so I think we can assume Mrs Murrell was killed only because of what she overheard."

"*Only!*"

"OK, I take your point. Fulbourn hasn't been able to work out what's going on. He's going to work on it tonight and Marcus may be able to tell me more tomorrow."

"So I have to go through with it?"

"You don't *have* to do anything, Jo. We can go tonight if you like."

"No, it's all right." I looked at his face. The bastard had known I wouldn't take him up on it. "But I want to be out of here by Wednesday night at the absolute latest."

He nodded slowly. "Fair enough. That gives us three more days. Assuming Fulbourn doesn't come up with the goods before then."

"How did Marcus manage to tell you all that on an open line?" I asked.

He grinned. "He and I can nearly always work out what the other's on about. Instead of cases, he referred to the firms I was worried about. Only one has cancelled the contract, and so on."

We walked in the grounds to watch the sunset again and went to bed at eleven. Not surprisingly, I couldn't sleep, even after taking a sleeping pill. After an hour, I called softly to him. He must have been lying awake too, because he came over straight away.

"Worried about tomorrow?"

"Tom, I'm terrified. Please hold me."

It was strange, needing his physical closeness so much and yet having no sexual desire, so different from the last time he'd comforted me all those months ago. This time it was he who was aroused and I who couldn't respond.

I did what I could for him and curiously, it gave us both release. He stayed with me until I slept.

Seventeen

Monday was pretty much a non-day. It wasn't that nothing happened, the very opposite in fact, only I was unaware of most of it.

I heard Tom get up and go for his run. I hoped against hope that even at this late stage, the Prof would have worked out what was going on and we could do a flit. This, however, was not to be.

Tom came back after half an hour, as red-faced as before, and turned on the radio.

"Well, I've got the spunk," he wheezed, "but not much else."

I waited while he recovered a little.

"Fulbourn says that what we've given him are medical notes, observations on the medical progress of a group of patients. He says he thinks there must be some complementary scientific notes, and he needs to look at those. And they'll be in Carla's room."

"Oh no! We'll never get away with another break-in."

"I know that."

"So what do we do?"

"We've still got three days. I'll work something out."

"Did he say anything about why the laparoscopies are taking so long?"

"No. We don't know for sure how many of the others did take that long – we only know about Mrs Murrell and Denny. Fulbourn says that the reasons given by Kent could, in theory, be the truth."

"So I've just got to take whatever comes," I said bitterly.

"Jo, I'll be here all the time. If your op goes on for too long, I'll be asking them why. And I'll be here with you all the time afterwards, to make sure nothing happens to you then."

I shrugged. "Sure. You'd better get showered and go down for your breakfast."

He gave a tight smile and disappeared into the bathroom. I was trying to make him feel guilty and we both knew it, but it was *my* head on the chopping block.

I lay back and tried to lose myself in the music after he'd gone. It was something by Schubert, but I wasn't in the mood. It seemed an age before he was back, although it wasn't much over half an hour.

"Denny's up and very breezy," he said, either trying to cheer me up or assuage his guilt. "I told her you were worried and she said she'd call in and see you."

Which she did a few minutes later. She was certainly very relaxed, even laid back, and despite everything, she did cheer me up. She stayed until Nurse Jenni came to give me the pre-med at ten.

Pethidine's a funny drug. It's the same every time (I'd had it myself, before my appendectomy, besides watching its effect on others). You're convinced it's not having any effect on you, and it's only when they come to wheel you away to the theatre that you realise you just don't care any more. The thought even went through my mind as the lift went down that this is what it must be like for a condemned murderer being taken for the lethal injection, but even as the anaesthetist (an old boy with a craggy, kindly face) stepped forward to administer the *coup de grace*, I wasn't worried, only detached. Count to ten, he said. I think I got to six.

Awakening from anaesthesia is also odd, much odder than awakening from sleep. Past and present are all jumbled up – my first sensation was of abdominal pain and I thought, damn! I've started my period, they'll cancel the op and I'll have to go through the whole business again. Then I heard Tom's voice, gentle, but also urgent.

"It's all right Jo, don't try to talk, it's all over and you're fine."

His face coalesced above me, and behind it, Nurse Jenni's. She removed Tom, checked me over, told me the abdominal pains were due to the air that had been pumped into me during the laparoscopy, and declared me fit.

Tom took my hand, told me again not to say anything and I wondered what he was so het up about. Nurse Jenni left us to it. It was comforting knowing that it was all over and he was there and I slid gratefully back into semi-consciousness.

Music, Tom and wakefulness, this time complete. I looked at the bedside clock – nearly four.

"How long was I out?" I asked him.

"Just over three hours, before you came round the first time."

"The same as Denny, then?"

He nodded. "I asked Leila after two hours why it was taking so long. She said she'd make enquiries, then came back with the answer that your eggs were in an awkward position."

I rubbed my still tender abdomen and felt the stitches. "Is it relevant? The fact that these ops are taking so long."

"I don't know. I can't see how."

Neither could I. Another thought came to me.

"Tom, when I was coming to, you kept on at me not to say anything – was I saying anything?"

He grinned. "I'll say you were. Tell the buggers I want twenty thousand was the most startling."

"Did I say that?"

"Several times. Obviously, you don't remember."

I told him about thinking I'd have to go through it again. "That's obviously where it came from."

"Mm. Gives you an idea of how Mrs Murrell might have given things away."

I shuddered. "Don't."

136

"Sorry. How *are* you feeling? Want anything to eat?"

I shook my head. "Not yet. My tummy hurts too much. Please don't go." I thought I'd felt him stirring.

"I'll stay with you as long as you like."

Nurse Jenni came back and told me the pain would be gone by tomorrow, and that I could have a light meal in bed this evening, if I felt like it. Told me I must relax. I told Tom I wished I could have ten thousand for every time I'd heard that; after she'd gone, of course.

The light meal consisted of scrambled eggs on toast, which I had before Tom went down for dinner. After that, we watched TV until about ten thirty. I didn't think sleep would come easily after being unconscious for so much of the day, but it did.

The next day, I was again awakened by Tom going out for his run. I felt much better, although still rather drowsy. Nurse Jenni came in and made me take some pills.

"Dr Kent would like to see you at nine thirty," she told me. "You can go down for breakfast first if you like, so long as you take things easily."

"Thanks, I will."

"Your husband certainly takes his jogging seriously," she observed.

"Don't I know it," I said with what I hoped was the right touch of bitterness. Then, more quietly, "I'm hoping a baby might substitute – to some extent, anyway."

"I'm sure it will," she said, rather mechanically, I thought.

We sat with Denny and Geoff at breakfast. Denny asked me how I was feeling and I said fine.

"Funny us both needing laparoscopies," she said.

"Isn't it? Did you ever have to have one before you came here?"

She shook her head. "Not to have eggs collected, no. Ultrasound's much less unpleasant, but if a laparoscopy's what it takes . . ." She shrugged and left the sentence unfinished.

She was still very relaxed and I wondered whether Dr Kent's pills were responsible.

"When are you leaving?" I asked.

"Tomorrow, probably. I'm due to have the embryos replaced in the morning." She held up crossed fingers. "Here's hoping."

I held mine up as well. "You and me both," I said, and suddenly felt a fraud.

Back in our room, I brushed my teeth and tidied up before going to see Dr Kent.

"What are your plans?" I asked Tom.

"Thought I'd pop out for a spell." He lowered his voice. "See Marcus."

I nodded.

"See you later, then," he said. "Be good."

In her room, Dr Kent quickly examined me and said I was doing well.

"We'll replace your eggs on either Thursday or Friday," she said. "We'll be monitoring both you and the eggs to see which is best. Meanwhile, do as little as possible. I want you to continue with the sedative I prescribed."

"Oh. Is that what the nurse gave me this morning?" I asked, remembering.

"Yes, that's right."

"Oh," I said again. "You think a sedative's necessary?"

"I think it helps, yes. I can't emphasise enough how important it is for you to relax at this stage. Your – *our* – success could depend on it."

"I see. In that case, fine." Like hell it was.

I returned to my room and lay on the bed, although not to sleep. I don't know what the drug was, but it induced a spurious sense of lazy well-being rather than drowsiness. I'm not taking any more, I thought.

I must have dozed off for a little, however, because Tom woke me at about half-past one.

"D'you want any lunch?" he asked. "We'd better hurry if you do."

"Not really," I said, yawning. "But I suppose I'd better. Did you—"

He put his finger to his lips and nodded. "After lunch," he mouthed.

We saw the Dacies coming out, but otherwise, we had the dining room to ourselves. I still wasn't feeling very hungry, but forced a little down for form's sake.

Back in our room, he turned on the musical backcloth and sat on the side of his bed. I sat beside him.

"I had quite a long talk with Marcus," he began. "And he had a long talk himself with Fulbourn on the phone last night. It seems that the data we found has thrown up a lot more questions than answers."

"Well, there's a surprise."

He reached into his inside pocket and pulled out a sheaf of papers. "Here's what Marcus gave me." He unfolded them and looked at the top sheet. "Of the cases in the earlier folders we found, the Stimulated DNA and Replaced DNA, none involved—"

"Does he know yet what those terms mean?"

"No, although he thinks they refer to the treatment of the sperm before it is injected into the egg. May I continue?"

"By all means."

"Thank you. Of these cases, none involved laparoscopies and all were failures, bar one of the replaced cases – she's about six months pregnant."

"But they've stopped doing those now."

"So it seems. Those cases, plus the Nuclear DNA cases, represent about fifteen per cent of Kent's work over the whole period. So far, all but that one have been failures, and yet the other eighty-five per cent of her work has been so successful as to make the overall success rate acceptable."

"So why is she bothering?"

"Why indeed? Now, looking more closely at the Nuclear DNA cases. There are twenty-five in all, not counting you and Denny. Of these, the first sixteen did not involve laparoscopies, and all were failures. The subsequent nine have all involved laparoscopy. All of these were also failures, ultimately, but one woman *did* become pregnant, although she then had a miscarriage during the first trimester of pregnancy."

"Curiouser and curiouser."

"Isn't it? And can you guess who that woman was?"

I felt my mouth drop open. "Oh no, not Denny?"

He slowly nodded. "And now she's back again . . . for another laparoscopy."

I closed my eyes to think. "Tom, of the eighty-five per cent not included in the folders, what proportion is by microinjection?"

"About half."

"And it's reasonably successful?"

"It's highly successful, more so here than anywhere else."

"So we come back to the question, why is she bothering? I mean" – I continued quickly – "this fifteen per cent, it's got to be some form of experimentation, hasn't it?"

"I'd say so, although Marcus still doesn't agree."

"But why experiment, if she's so successful anyway?"

"I don't know. That's what I meant by more questions than answers."

I shivered suddenly. "Tom, that means she's intending to experiment on *me*."

He put an arm round me. "Not necessarily. Marcus is still of the opinion that money is behind it. He says that some of the apparently successful microinjections could simply be carefully selected donor inseminations, carried out after microinjection has failed."

"But we've already been over that, what about the risk of discovery?"

"I agree with you. But in your case, Jo, even if it is some form of experimentation, you'll be out of here before they can try it on you."

"What about poor Denny?"

"Well, unpleasant though it is for her, the only woman to

have actually come to any harm was Mrs Murrell, and we know why."

"It's still horrible."

"Oh, I agree. There's one other thing. Fulbourn has checked through his own records and noticed that all the women, with the sole exception of Denny, who figured in the fifteen per cent have subsequently turned up in the other eighty-five per cent, after just one experimental treatment. Assuming that's what it is."

"As though they're experimented on once, then put on to conventional treatment?" I said slowly. "Except Denny . . . because the experiment was a partial success?"

"Exactly. Look" – he shuffled through the sheets of paper – "these are copies of what we photographed, and here we have Wendy Dacie," he pointed, "and here, Alison Purton – that's the other couple staying at the moment. Both were in the Nuclear DNA file last time, neither of them became pregnant, and neither are in the file this time."

"But they might have been added, after Denny and me."

"Nope. They're not having laparoscopies."

"How do you know that?"

"I found out yesterday. Used my charm."

"So the crucial question is," I said after a pause, "what is actually being done to the fifteen per cent, the women in the folders?"

"We're not going to find that out without getting into Carla's room."

I groaned. "I don't see how we can."

"Well, we certainly can't at night, but that doesn't mean we can't try during the day."

I stared at him. "But they'll be there."

"Not when they go to lunch."

"But they might not go together. Besides, even if they did, they'd reactivate the alarm."

"They don't go together."

"How do you know?"

"I watched them, yesterday and today, before I came up to you. Carla goes at twelve and comes back at a quarter to one. Chrystal goes at one, so the alarm won't be reactivated, since there's always one of them there. All we have to do is make sure Chrystal's attention is engaged while I break into Carla's room."

"Oh, that's all is it? And I don't like the sound of we."

"There is a way, and it's quite simple. Can you draw?"

"*Draw*? What's that got to do with anything?"

"Can you?"

"A bit, but—"

"Come into the garden, Jo, and I'll show you."

"No."

"Jo, there isn't any other way, I've looked." His face was pinched and there was the slightest edge of desperation in his voice. "We're not going to get anywhere by doing nothing."

"I'm sorry, I won't do it."

"Why not? We could be out of here by tomorrow afternoon."

"It's too risky. What if you were caught?"

"I won't be . . ." He tailed off as I went into a spasm of coughing.

We were behind the rhododendron bushes, and I was smoking one of his cheroots. I hadn't brought my cigarettes with me and it was the first tobacco I'd had for nearly forty hours. It had even crossed my mind to try and give it up – until he'd told me what he wanted me to do.

"I won't be caught," he said.

"There's no guarantee of that."

"There never is a guarantee, but it's very unlikely."

His idea was for me to bring a chair out on to the lawn and sketch the back of the manor. From that position, Chrystal was clearly visible so long as she remained in the partitioned section of the lab where she seemed to carry out most of her work. I was to start sketching before twelve. When Carla left for lunch, Tom would glance through the back door at me. If I was sitting, it meant Chrystal was inside the partition. If she left it, I was to stand up. He'd unlock Carla's door, immediately lock the connecting door to the lab, then search for and photograph the relevant files.

"I could be out in less than three minutes," he said. "All I have to do is glance out at you occasionally. So long as you're sitting, fine. If you stand up, I get out quick."

"How are you going to see me if you're down on the floor photographing files?"

"I'll keep glancing up at you, as I said. If Chrystal does move, it'll still take her at least a couple of minutes to de-gown and get to the connecting door, even if that's where she's going. If the worst came to the worst, she'd find it locked and I'd still have time to get out."

"Leaving a locked door to explain."

He shrugged. "If I'd got what I wanted, we could ske-daddle."

"But what if Carla came back and found you photographing her files?"

He sighed. "That is a risk, albeit a small one. If it did happen, I'd have to hold her up and we'd get out."

"I'm sorry, Tom," I said again, "but it's too risky. No."

He sighed. "That leaves us with two alternatives. One, we leave empty-handed. Two, we subdue Cal again tomorrow night, then take the files before we leave."

I know. I could have opted for leaving empty-handed, but would I have still got the ten thousand? So I allowed him to talk me round. I started sketching that afternoon (the bastard had already bought pad and pencils) to get them used to the idea. To my surprise, I rather enjoyed it.

Eighteen

I couldn't sleep again that night. Tom was snoring, which was unusual for him. Or maybe I'd just been asleep when he'd done it before. I wondered for a moment whether it might have been better to have taken the sedative pill that evening rather than spitting it out when Nurse Sophi had gone. No, I still didn't know what was in them.

At last, I got up, took one of my own sleeping pills and went into the bathroom for a smoke while I waited for it to work.

Viewed rationally, I had to admit that Tom's scheme didn't seem quite so insane in that it carried no more risk than our previous escapade and there were no better alternatives. I was still dreading it, though.

God, it'll be marvellous to be out of here, I thought. Denny and Geoff had been 'demob happy', as Tom had called it, at dinner. Well, in twenty-four hours at the latest, we'd be on our way. Just the small matter of Carla's experimental data to find and photograph first. If it existed.

Tom was still snoring when I went back in. I gave him a shove and he turned over and stopped. Mumbled something in his sleep. I stood, looking down at him for a few moments. How did I really feel about him? He'd certainly been his own bloody self, but I knew I'd miss him once this was over. A lump came to my throat; I went back to bed and tried to swallow it. Mercifully, sleep came quite quickly.

Morning . . . Tom going for his run . . . Nurse Jenni giving me the pill and me pretending to take it. Denny and Geoff at breakfast . . .

"This is it then, Denny," I said to her.

"Sure is." Her smile mellowed out. "Let me have your address before we go, and I'll let you know how I get on. You must let me know, as well."

"Of course." Smiling back at her was one of the hardest things I'd ever done, knowing how unlikely it was that she was pregnant with their baby.

After breakfast, I went outside and sketched the manor from the front a couple of times to keep up the image, before moving to the back again, where it was more sheltered. Oddly enough, the cleaner lines of the back of the building (without the wistaria) were more satisfying to draw.

"Not bad, Mrs Jones."

"Dr Kent – you startled me." I hadn't sensed her approach at all.

"I'm sorry. I came out to say I'd like to examine you again later this afternoon – shall we say five?"

"Yes, fine."

"Good. I'll see you then." She made her way to the back door.

An hour or so later, Tom came out with Denny and Geoff, who were leaving and wanted to say goodbye.

"That's lovely, Jo," said Denny, looking at my pad. "Didn't I see you earlier doing one of the front?"

I showed her, then on impulse, tore it out and gave it to her. "Something to remember me by."

"Thank you, Jo." She put her hands on my shoulders and kissed my cheek. "You will let us know how you get on, won't you? Tom's got our address."

"Of course. Good luck, Denny."

After they'd gone, I shook my head to try and clear away the sadness, then started on a new sheet.

Twelve o'clock . . .

I continued sketching, or tried to. Chrystal was working in the partition. I saw Carla stand up, take off her white coat and hang it up before leaving her room. A couple of minutes later, Tom appeared momentarily at the back door before disappearing again. A minute later, Carla's door opened and he reappeared briefly before ducking out of sight.

Chrystal continued working. I continued pretending to, although my hand was shaking far too much to draw.

Hurry up, damn you, I thought. My jaw ached because my teeth were clenched so tight. Tom's head bobbed up and down again.

Chrystal still continued working.

"That's nice," a voice said behind me and I let out a shriek.

"I'm sorry, madam. I didn't mean to scare you." It was the gardener-cum-heavy.

"I – it's all right. I – I was absorbed, that's all." Surely, he'd hear the tremor in my voice.

"Would you do one for me? I'd pay you." He was standing quite close, I could smell the physical work on him, see the bleeper device clipped on to his belt and his name badge, which said he was called Brian.

"Oh, I couldn't" – Chrystal shut the door of the incubator, walked quickly into the gowning lobby and stripped off her gown and mask – "I couldn't take any money." Remembering what I was there for, I shot to my feet, holding my pencil vertically at arm's length as though measuring the building.

Tom, where *are* you?

"But I'd like to," Brian said.

Brian would see Tom when he next popped up. I turned, faced him and smiled, willing him to look at me. "Besides, I'm afraid we might be leaving tomorrow, so there wouldn't really be time."

"Oh. All right, then." His disappointment was palpable.

"I suppose I could try and do one this afternoon for you."

"Would you?"

"I'll try. Would you prefer the view from the back or front?"

"Oh, the front, please. And you must let me pay you."

My face cracked in a smile. "Well, if you insist . . ."
"I do."
"Will you be here this afternoon?"
"I'll be around till about five."
"Then I'll look for you out here before that."
"Thank you, madam." He actually touched his forelock, and went back to his work.

Had he seen anything? I was as sure as I could be he hadn't. I glanced back up at the window.

Dr Kent and Carla were now standing together in Carla's room, looking out at me. I forced myself to smile and wave, and after a moment. Dr Kent waved back. I sat down again. Chrystal was back in the partition.

I swallowed, pretending to draw. Where was Tom?

I looked up again to measure a perspective with my pencil. Dr Kent and Carla were now in the lab, Carla talking on what looked like an intercom to Chrystal.

Where was Tom?

As though in answer, he appeared in the doorway and sauntered over to me, peering over my shoulder.

"How's it going?"

I smiled up at him. "What happened, Tom?"

"Keep drawing for another quarter of an hour, then come up to the suite." He bent and kissed my cheek and was gone.

The minutes crawled by. Dr Kent and Carla went back to Carla's room and talked. Carla bent down, to the safe, I assumed. Chrystal degowned, put her head round the door, then left, for her lunch, probably. I looked at my watch again.

At last, the fifteen minutes were up, I packed my things away and went to our room. Tom was lying on his bed, listening to the radio.

"What happened?" I asked.

"I'm not quite sure myself," he said. "I'd got the safe open and the folders were there, I saw them. I pulled out the one marked Nuclear DNA, opened it, then took a quick look at you before getting the camera out, and saw you standing with the gardener."

"His name's Brian."

"Brian. Well, I wondered at first whether Brian was the reason you were standing, so I shoved the folder back anyway and relocked the safe. Just as well I did. I'd unlocked the connecting door and was on my way to the other door when I heard a key rattling in it and Carla's and Kent's voices outside. I knew it would take them a few seconds to work out why the key wouldn't unlock the door, so I went through the connecting door, planning to tell Chrystal I was looking for Carla. Well, Chrystal was in the partition and didn't see me, so I ducked down and went out of the lab door and into the corridor. Fortunately, by this time, Kent and Carla had gone into her room, so I quickly scarpered. He let out a sigh. "Close, eh?""

"Too close." I told him how they'd stared out at me and then questioned Chrystal. "Tom, I've had enough."

"But the files are *there*, Jo. I saw them. We're that far away." He held his fingers up a quarter of an inch apart.

"OK, tell Marcus that and get him to arrange a raid on the place – surely we've got enough for that?"

"Yes, we have."

"So arrange it and let's get out, now."

"No."

I stared at him.

"Because we couldn't arrange it in time. We'd have to get a warrant for an official search, and the very earliest that could be done would be for tomorrow afternoon. By which time you might well have had eggs replaced."

"But why can't we just – Oh, I see. If we clear out before then . . ."

"Kent will guess why and either destroy or hide the evidence before the search takes place." Tom finished for me.

"But I thought you said we already have enough evidence."

"Fulbourn has worked out enough to justify a search, and

probably enough to show malpractice and deception as well, but he hasn't unravelled the whole thing yet. They could only be prosecuted on comparatively minor charges, and a good counsel might even get them off. We *must* have Carla's files."

"But how are we going to get them?"

"We'll take them on our way out tonight."

"How?"

"We immobilise Cal, take them and go."

"Oh no, not the dart gun again."

"No, I'll simply tell him to stick 'em up."

"But he'll know who we are."

"They'll know that anyway when they find us missing."

"Supposing the files don't contain enough to—"

"They will, I'm sure of it."

"But suppose they don't," I persisted. "We could be charged with assault and goodness knows what."

"Almost certainly not. Marcus says that since there's already enough to warrant an official search, he could justify this, so long as we don't harm anybody."

"Is almost good enough?"

"Marcus has authorised it and that's good enough for me. There's no way I'm going to leave this job unfinished."

So that was that.

The rest of the day was pure bell. I picked at my lunch (he ate with gusto), then we adjourned to the bushes. I took one of my sketches to give to Brian, but there was no sign of him.

I gobbled down some smoke. "If they catch us," I said, blowing it out, "they'd have nothing to lose from killing us."

"They would, actually."

"They've already killed once."

"A killing which, unfortunately, we'll probably never be able to prove. If they killed us, they would be nailed, and they'd know it. Were they to catch us, which they won't, they'd simply destroy the evidence and then say prove it."

"Or use us as hostages."

"Why should they? It's not in that league. Besides, very few villains get away with that, and they'll know it."

He always had to know best.

We found Brian working in the garden on the way back and I presented him with the sketch.

"It's one I did earlier today," I said. "I hope that's all right."

"Just what I wanted," he said, looking at it. "Now you must let me—" he put his hand in his pocket.

"No." I said. "A gift. I insist."

He glanced at Tom. "OK. Thank you, madam."

By the time we got back to our room, it was almost time for me to see Dr Kent. I brushed my teeth, showered and changed (thank God I won't have to do this every time I have a smoke any more) and made my way down.

Her examination was much more thorough than usual, in more ways than one. She took my blood pressure, pulse rate and temperature, then listened to my heart and lungs.

"Is drawing something that's always interested you?" she asked suddenly.

"I – er – yes, when I was younger, very much so. I even thought about art as a career at one stage." You're gabbling. I told myself. "I still sometimes wonder whether I made the right decision . . ."

"Hmm. Your blood pressure and pulse rate are higher than they should be," she said. "You have been taking the tablets I prescribed?"

"Oh, yes." I paused. "I have felt rather nervous about being here, as you know. Perhaps that's why . . ."

"Perhaps it is." Her piercing grey eyes seemed to be probing my mind. "Now, I'm going to give you a scan."

"A scan?"

"Yes. I want to see how your ovaries have settled down. It could influence when I replace your eggs."

I couldn't see how, but I went through to the scanning room and slowly undressed. I hadn't liked the tone of the conversation at all.

She took a long time over the scan, studying the screen intently, nodding her head now and again.

"Very good," she said at last, her voice filled with satisfaction, even excitement. "Excellent. I shall almost certainly replace your eggs tomorrow." She looked at me a little less severely. "Try to have a good night's sleep tonight and I'll examine you again first thing in the morning."

Back in our room, I told Tom what had happened. "I didn't like the way she looked at me at all. I'm sure she suspects something."

"Possibly, but not enough for her to act on," he said thoughtfully. "Not yet, anyway. It's as well we're going tonight."

We spent the time until dinner sorting out what things to take with us, since we obviously wouldn't be able to take much. Tom had already found an excuse to turn the car round so that it was facing the right way.

The other two couples seemed to have broken the ice and were sharing a table at dinner, and it was we who were alone. It was then I realised how much I missed Denny, and even Geoff.

Nineteen

We left it till just after one, then Tom shrugged himself into his backpack and we set off. Gently pulling the door to, behind us, we crept along the dimly lit passage, avoiding the creaking floorboard. We reached the top landing. The floor of the hall gleamed dully. I don't know why, but the thought of confronting Cal face to face scared me more than anything and I couldn't stop trembling.

Tom tied the rope to the banister as before and lowered himself over. I followed.

I was about halfway down when there was a noise from the desk below and a voice said. "OK, hold it right there."

Brian. He had a gun.

"Come down, madam," he said, his eyes still on Tom.

"I – I can't. I'm stuck." My hands were frozen on to the rope.

He glanced up at me and Tom hit him on the point of the jaw so fast that it didn't register at first. Brian lurched against the panelling; Tom caught him before he fell and lowered him to the floor.

"Come on," he hissed, slipping along the passage under the stairs.

My hands unfroze and I lowered myself down. Brian lay still as still. I went through to the passage just in time to see Tom disappear round the corner.

"Don't move a muscle, Cal."

I reached the corner. Cal had come out of the security room and Tom had his gun trained on him.

"OK, back inside," Tom said, "sit down . . . hands behind you . . . Jo, you know what to do."

He moved to let me through. Cal was on his seat. I pulled the plastic cuffs from my pocket and said. "Put your hands behind your back, one—"

"What if I don't?" He'd recovered himself. His voice was an unpleasant drawl.

"You've seen this," – Tom touched the silencer on the end of his gun – "that's what."

"You ain't got the guts," Cal sneered.

In a flash, Tom had the gun levelled at his kneecap. Cal shrugged and pushed his hands between the two supports of the backrest.

"One of your hands the other side of the support," I said.

For a moment I thought be was going to refuse, then his hand came slowly round.

"Closer together."

"I can't."

"Out of the way, Jo."

"OK. OK." Cal's hands came together and I snapped the cuffs round his wrists. They only just fit.

Tom said quietly, "We've been set up. Time we called for help." He picked up the phone and started keying in numbers, then swore and turned back on Cal. "How d'you get a line?"

Cal stared back at him with mute hatred.

Tom thrust the gun into his throat. "I said, how d'you get a line?" he repeated gratingly.

Still Cal said nothing, and for a moment, I thought Tom was going to hit him, even shoot him, then he handed me the gun and quickly gagged Cal with a handkerchief.

"Come on." He bustled me through the door and pulled it shut behind him.

"What about Brian?"

He hesitated. "Haven't got any more cuffs, he'll be all right."

We went down the passage to Carla's room, which Tom unlocked.

"Tom . . ."

"I'm not going without these." He found another key and unlocked the safe. "They've bloody gone!"

He jumped up, pushed open the window and climbed out. turning to help me. A gibbous moon hung in the sky. We ran along the path past the laboratory, through the gate to the car park.

"Bloody *hell!*" he breathed. The two front tyres of the Astra were flat. He looked round. "There's another Vauxhall – there." He ran over to a Cavalier, undid the backpack and pulled out the screwdriver and inserted it into the lock and turned, his face straining in the moonlight. There was a crack as it gave. He pulled open the door and looked round again.

"I need a lever – iron bar, wooden post, anything – try over there." He pointed to a shed and went over to the garage.

I opened the shed door. "Will this do?" I asked, showing him a garden hoe with an iron handle.

"Yeah." He threaded it through the spokes of the steering wheel and pulled. There was another crack as the lock snapped. I glanced back at the upper windows, but no lights came on. Tom dropped the hoe on to the gravel and flung the pack on to the back seat before sliding behind the wheel and opening the passenger door.

"Get in."

I pulled it closed as gently as I could. Tom felt underneath the steering wheel, pulled out a circular piece of metal with wires attached, inserted his own key somewhere in the middle and twisted . . . The engine turned over, fired, caught. He found reverse and gently backed out.

"Tom, it's Cal . . ."

He'd appeared from the front of the house. Tom spun the wheel and turned down the drive. I twisted round. Cal raised his arm and I thought he was going to shoot us, then he lowered his arm and ran to the garage.

"Where are we going?"

"We've been set up," he snarled. "The gate at the top will be locked."

"Look out!" The wooden gate ahead gleamed in the moonlight.

"Hold on."

He drove straight at the gate. It leapt at us, filling the screen and shattering in front of my eyes. Then we were racing up a slight rise and descending into the valley beyond, the clattering of the suspension mingled with the slap and scratch of vegetation.

"We've lost a headlamp," he said. I hadn't noticed.

The track switched, climbed steeply. The engine laboured, then we were going down again. The scrubby trees grew thicker, closing in . . .

"Where are we going?" I asked again.

"Anywhere. We need a metalled road to get us to one of the villages."

The front wheels hit something, the car heaved and there was a crunch from underneath as we grounded, followed by a ragged growl.

"Exhaust pipe," shouted Tom.

The track climbed again, the engine sounded terrible and we slowed. I glanced behind.

"We're being followed!"

"I know." He changed down, the engine revved, sounding more like an aircraft as the wheels slipped in some mud. We were down to a jog as we breasted the rise. Something suddenly loomed overhead. I screamed, then realised it was the barrel of one of the wrecked tanks we'd seen – how long ago?

I looked behind again, the lights were closer, much closer.

"It's catching up."

"Yeah, it's the Range Rover."

I looked down into the valley ahead. A church tower, pale grey in the moonlight, rose from a group of trees, houses clustered below it.

"There's a village, just down there." I pointed. "We can get help."

"There can't be—"

Without warning, we burst onto a narrow metalled road.

"Right!" I shouted. "Go right."

He swung the wheel and we lurched round, gathering speed down a hill. After a couple of hundred yards, the handlamp picked out a sign: IMBER VILLAGE, and Tom gave a wild laugh.

"What's so bloody funny?" I yelled at him.

"You've taken us to a bloody ghost village, that's what."

Twenty

We roared down through a belt of trees, the church tower rearing above us surrounded by high posts and a chain link fence, down into the village. There were no lights, only churned up mud and debris, no pavements, no windows.

Tom swung the car off the road and tried to get behind one of the buildings, but the car become grounded and stalled.

Silence.

"Out."

He opened his door. We could hear the Range Rover coming fast down the hill.

"Over here." He grabbed my arm, dragging me across a clearing. I tripped over a furrow, but he hauled me up and over to a flat-roofed building marked Post Office. There were no doors or windows, only openings. He pushed me through and pulled me into the shadows.

The Range Rover stopped and its engine was switched off. Silence. It started up again and slowly moved on.

"Please God they don't see the car," breathed Tom.

The Range Rover stopped, then moved on again.

"They don't know which way we've gone, or whether we're still here," he whispered.

"Tom, where are we?"

"Imber. Right in the middle of Salisbury Plain. It was taken over by the army during the war and has been used for training ever since."

"Doesn't anyone live here?"

"No."

"Is there a phone?"

"There used to be, over by the old court, but I don't know if it's still there. We should have stayed put," he said savagely, "I could have made Cal tell us how the phone worked."

"But we didn't. Can we get to the phone here?"

"I'm just trying to get my bearings . . . I think so, yes."

"Well, let's go, before they come back."

"I go, you stay."

"I'm not staying here on my own."

"I'll stand a better chance on my own. I trained here, remember?"

He was right, as usual.

"If I don't come back, say after an hour, you'll have to try and get out on your own."

"I couldn't, I'm completely lost."

"Remember the road down into the village? If you follow that back up, past where we turned, I'm sure it leads to the main road."

"I couldn't walk that far in the dark."

"It's only about five or six miles, and there's a moon. Anyway, I will come back." He kissed my cheek quickly, then he was gone.

He was right about the moon, I could even make out the walls and floor of the building I was in now. The floor glistened. It would – I could feel the mud seeping through my shoes. Mud and what else? I swallowed and tried to move my feet, but it only made the wetness worse. There were noises, night noises I'd been completely unaware of before – an owl hooting, a scream in the distance, a vixen perhaps, and something scurrying past outside.

Oh, please God, not rats, I thought.

Keep hold of yourself, Josephine, you only get rats where people are living, don't you? Anyway, the scurrying had passed.

The vixen screamed again. What am I doing here? I thought, I could have paid that ten thousand off in time, if only I'd—

The Gift

If only. A bit late now.

Even Tom had come out with an 'if only', wishing he'd stayed and made Cal talk . . . but we hadn't realised how bad things were then. We'd been set up all right.

Wouldn't the noise we'd made have woken up some of the other patients, double glazing or not? No. Now I came to think of it, I'd never heard a single noise from outside. They'd all still be sound asleep in their nice warm beds.

Things must be bad for Tom to come out with 'if onlys'.

I tried to look at my watch but the light wasn't bright enough to see it by. I had no idea how much time had passed and I'd have given anything for a smoke, but that would be asking for it.

I could head rustlings and squeakings outside. A village of animals and ghosts – the very word made me look round nervously. No – I smiled wryly to myself – the squaddies and the gunfire would have driven any self-respecting spooks out by now.

More animal noises. I swallowed. Time passed, at least, I supposed it must have.

My feet and legs were growing numb with cold and stillness. I tried to shift them, but they were stuck. For a moment I panicked – then they came free with a revolting sucking noise.

It was no good, I had to look at my watch, and if I was going to do that, I might as well have a cigarette.

I listened carefully, then put a cigarette in my mouth, flicked my lighter and looked at my watch. Some small animal scampered away in alarm.

Was it really only five-past two? Then I realised I didn't even know what time Tom had left.

The smoke tasted wonderful, so wonderful that I had another, although it didn't solve any problems.

Time crawled on. It was now nearly twenty minutes since I'd last looked at my watch, and at least another twenty before that that Tom had gone. He wasn't coming back, which meant they had him, they were out there somewhere and I was alone.

159

The thought was so appalling that my head buzzed and I felt my control slipping away.

No, hang on, I'd have heard something if they'd caught him, wouldn't I? Maybe he'd spotted them and was lying low, maybe he'd run into them after he'd found the phone, in which case, maybe . . .

Did they already know where I was? Had they seen my lighter? You idiot! But I hadn't heard any noises other than animal, not the Range Rover . . . or had I?

I thought back. No.

If they had caught Tom, they still couldn't know where I was, or they'd have come for me by now. I'd have to give Tom a bit longer, then . . . Then what?

The thought of staying here was unbearable, the thought of moving even worse. But I couldn't stay here indefinitely, it would be dawn in a couple of hours. I'd have to go. Soon.

The thought made me tremble all over again.

I'd have to move.

The Range Rover was somewhere on the other side of the village and I hadn't heard anyone, so if I did what Tom told me, maybe I'd have a chance.

I had to move.

I took a breath, pulled my feet from the mud and made my way over to the door.

The moon was still high, flooding the village with ethereal light. The churned-up mud and stark eyeless buildings were like something out of Beirut or Bosnia; the branches and leaves of the trees and the sky were like something out of a nightmare Disney.

Another breath. I stepped out, picking my way across the furrows and trying to remember which way we'd come. There was the car, paintwork glinting in the moonlight. Could I take that?

No. Even if I managed to start it, the noise would be audible for miles, but at least I could see which way we'd come now. I hurried between the hateful flat-roofed buildings – how could I have ever mistaken this for a real village? – over to the clump of trees by the road, and hid in their shadows.

Not a sound, just the leaves above rustling in the breeze.

I started up the side of the road, my feet brushing dead leaves; past the church, its tower black, silhouetted against the sky. No sounds, just the breeze and me, both shuffling leaves.

A twig cracked and I froze. I couldn't tell where it came from.

I swallowed and moved further into the shadows. Someone leapt from the deeper shadows, pinioning my arms. It was Brian's voice shouting, "Over here. I've got her, over here. It's all right madam, we're not going to hurt you."

"You fucking moron," I heard myself shriek. I tried to kick him, but he was too strong . . .

Then others arrived and a torch flashed.

"Hold on to her!" It was Dr Kent's voice. "Hold her *still*!

Brian's arms tightened, I screamed and kicked as someone grabbed my legs, Cal, I think, then there was a sharp pain in my buttock and I thought, *The lethal injection*.

Then I stopped being scared and my last thoughts were of regret for leaving my mother behind.

Twenty-One

L imbo.
  I lay, aware of myself only in the abstract, not wanting it any other way.

Discomfort. I tried to push it away, to cling to limbo, but gradually, discomfort took over and I opened my eyes.

I was lying in bed in a dimly lit room. I needed the loo. My mouth felt very dry and tasted unpleasant. I pushed the duvet aside, sat up and swung my legs over the side of the bed, and immediately felt so dizzy I had to lie down again.

There was something attached to my left wrist. With eyes still closed, I felt for it with my other hand. It was a bracelet of some sort with tubing attached. I opened my eyes and peered at it – it was one of Tom's plastic handcuffs and the 'tubing' was plastic covered wire that led somewhere across the floor.

The shock of this unclogged my memory banks – our escape from the manor . . . Imber . . . oblivion. Where was Tom?

I sat up, panicking, on the point of shouting his name, then stopped myself. I was alive, but why? Was Tom still alive?

Sitting up had increased the pressure on my bladder to the point where I had to attend to it. I eased my legs over the side of the bed again (I was in my own nightdress, I noticed) and cautiously stood up. Again, there was a rush of dizziness, but I took a few slow, deep breaths and gradually, it subsided.

The light, although dim, was enough for me to make out a bedside cabinet with a plastic jug and glass, and a door on the other side of the room. I cautiously walked over and tried it but it was locked. Even if it hadn't been, I wouldn't have been able to go through it because of the cuff. By now my need was desperate and I was about to bang on the door when I noticed an armchair near the foot of the bed with a chamber pot beside it, its top covered by a tea-towel.

My nose wrinkled in disgust and I turned back to the door when it occurred to me that it might be an idea to examine the room on my own before calling anyone.

I used the chamber pot, covered it again with the towel, then drank several glasses of water from the jug, noticing as I did so that my left arm was slightly sore. I held it up. It was bruised on the inside, and there was a plaster, presumably where I'd been on some kind of drip.

The light can't always be this dim, I thought, and went over to the door again. Beside it was a dimmer switch which I used to turn up the light.

The room was about fifteen feet square and obviously in an attic of some sort, because the ceiling was pitched on three sides. A single window of the Velux type was fitted flush with the roof. I tried opening it, but it was jammed closed and shuttered on the outside. I dimmed the light and a chink of brightness round the edge of the window suggested daylight outside.

I brightened the light again and looked round. On the far side of the room was a TV and video player, a music centre and a bookcase. Then I turned my attention to the wire that held me. It was about fifteen feet long with a built-in loop at each end. One loop was inside the single cuff on my wrist, while the other was hitched round the stout copper piping that ran from the radiator to the floor. I could move anywhere inside the room, but no further than the door, even if it was open.

At this point, something snapped and I found myself pummelling on the door with my fists, shouting over and over. "Let me out. Let me out. Let me *out*!"

Heavy footsteps came running up the stairs and a voice, called, "OK, OK, button it, Dr Kent's just coming."

A key turned in the lock, a bolt was drawn and the door opened to reveal Dr Kent, and behind her, Cal.

"May I come in please, Mrs Jones?" she said.

I swallowed and shrugged.

"I'm hardly in a position to stop you." I turned and walked back to the bed and sat down on the edge.

"Wait on the landing, please, Calvin," she said. "I'll call you if I need you."

"Yes, ma'am." He pulled the door to gently.

Dr Kent came in. She was holding her medical bag.

"May I sit down?" She indicated the chair.

"Be my guest."

She was dressed as she usually was, in sensible skirt, cream top and pearls.

"How are you feeling, Mrs Jones?"

"Where's Tom?"

"Safe and well."

"Where?"

"I couldn't tell you exactly. We released him."

I didn't know whether to be glad or sorry at this news. It didn't occur to me to disbelieve her.

"In that case, he'll find me."

"You must give up any idea of being found. You didn't answer my question. How are you feeling?"

"I'll survive."

"Good, that's exactly what I want you to do." She paused. "I take it that Jones isn't your real name?"

"No. It's Josephine Farewell."

"And Mr Jones?"

"That is his real name."

"I somehow thought it might be. Now, Miss – or is it Mrs – Farewell?"

"Miss."

"Good. It might have complicated things if there had been a Mr Farewell."

"Things are complicated enough already. There may be no

Mr Farewell, but there is the Department of Health, which sent me here with Mr Jones. They'll find me. In fact, I'm rather surprised they haven't done so already." As I said this, I realised that wherever we were, it couldn't be Catcott Manor.

"I'm not surprised at all. As I said just now, you must give up the idea of being found. Miss Farewell. If you want to continue surviving, that is."

"Why *am* I surviving, Dr Kent?"

"Because I want you to," she said, opening her bag. "I'm going to examine you. Please don't force me to ask for Calvin's assistance. I really don't want that." Her grey eyes held mine. For a moment I thought about resisting, then my will collapsed.

Best go along with her. I told myself.

"All right."

"Good. Lie on the bed, please." She took a stethoscope and a sphygmomanometer from her bag and measured my blood pressure, heart rate and temperature. Her professionalism was unaltered. She gently peeled away the plaster on my arm, examined the lesion underneath and said, "Good, it doesn't need another. Could you stay on the bed, please?"

She got up, went over to the door, opened it and said something to Cal. A moment later, to my astonishment, she wheeled in the ultrasound scanner. I was sure it was the one from Catcott.

She brought it level with the bed. It was humming and the screen glowed.

"Lie still." She gently pulled up my nightdress. "I'm going to scan you."

I shook my head slightly in bewilderment. "Why?"

She applied gel to my abdomen. "Keep still please." She picked up the sensor and slid it around as she watched the screen.

"Why are you doing this? Why am I here?"

"I will answer all your questions in time," she replied without looking up. "But not now. Not today."

165

"How long have I been here?"

"A day."

An appalling thought occurred to me.

"Dr Kent" – my voice trembled – "have you replaced eggs in me while I've been here?"

She stopped moving the sensor for a moment and looked up at me.

"No. Now please don't talk any more while I'm doing this."

I did as she asked and she studied the screen intently, grunting softly to herself now and again as she placed a cross on it. After about five minutes, she said, "Good" and put the sensor away. She wiped my belly with some tissue.

"I'll organise some breakfast for you. You must be feeling hungry by now."

"Not particularly. What I really need is a cigarette."

"So you weren't telling me the truth when you said you'd given up." She pulled my nightdress down and stood up. "Well, I'm afraid that's one thing I can't allow you to have."

"Why not?" I demanded.

She wheeled the scanner over to the door. "I'll be back shortly." The door closed behind her and the lock clicked.

What did she want with me? Where was I? Why?

Oh, how I wished Tom was here.

My throat swelled in the silence of the barren room and I felt my eyes prick and my face screw up. Tears trickled down the sides of my nose and I turned and buried my head in the pillow, gripping the sides, pushing them into my face as my body shook with sobs.

I didn't hear the door open, the first I knew of her presence was her hand on my shoulder and her voice.

"That's right, let it come out . . ."

I turned to put my arms round her, then realising what I was doing, I thrust myself away. For an instant, there had been a look of genuine compassion on her face, then it quickly resolved itself into its usual neutrality.

The Gift

"There are coffee and cereal on the table, I'll bring you a cooked breakfast in a minute." She got up and left the room.

The fact that I'd almost allowed myself to be comforted by her made me angry enough to stop crying. I was still thirsty and thought that if I couldn't smoke, I could at least have some caffeine – it might help me think. The coffee was at just the right temperature and tasted as though it had been recently ground. It was beautiful. I had another cup and tried to boot my brain into action.

Why was I here? I believed her about Tom; I thought I believed her about the eggs. But she'd scanned me. Why! unless she was monitoring me? And she'd said that cigarettes were one thing she couldn't allow me to have. Did that mean she had replaced eggs in me?

She'd said she would answer all my questions – in time. How much time? I wondered.

Could I escape? I looked down at the cuff on my wrist. Tom would certainly have tried. Perhaps I should try and think like him. So far, I'd only seen Dr Kent and Cal. Were the others here as well?

One thing was certain, there was nothing to be gained from deliberately antagonising her. I'd have to lull her into dropping her guard. Might as well start co-operating now.

On the tray were two small cereal packets, Bran and Corn Flakes respectively. I emptied the Bran Flakes into the bowl and added some milk. After the first spoonful I realised that I was hungry, ravenously. I was just finishing the Corn Flakes when the key rattled in the door (had they left it in? I wondered) and Dr Kent came in again, holding another tray.

"Hungry after all?" she said as she replaced the tray on the table. This one held eggs and bacon, beans and fried bread. My mouth watered.

"Yes, I am."

"Good, I'll leave you to it."

I polished it off and then poured some more coffee and looked round the room. There was a stack of videos beside

167

the video player. I looked through them – *Educating Rita, Hannah and her Sisters, Shirley Valentine*. I smiled wryly and wondered whether they were hers. I turned to the CDs. These were mostly classical, some Mozart and Beethoven, but a preponderance of French composers: Fauré, Debussy, Ravel, Satie.

I had just began to look at the books when the door opened again and Dr Kent came back in.

"Finished? Good. I'll clear these things away and then perhaps you'd like a bath?"

A bath? I glanced down at the cuff . . . that would mean releasing me, surely?

"Yes, I would, Dr Kent," I said humbly. "Thank you."

She looked at me quizzically for a moment before saying, "Good" again, then picked up the tray and the coffee pot and backed out.

She hadn't locked the door. I tiptoed quickly over, eased it open and peeped out. A short passage led to a landing on which Cal was standing, leaning against the wall and looking impassively back at me. The scanner was beside him. I shut the door and retreated to the bed. A couple of minutes later, Dr Kent came back.

"Are you decent?"

I shrugged. "As decent as I can be with just a nightdress."

"You can put this on in a moment." She held up a fleecy dressing gown. "I'm going to unlock you," she said. "Calvin has a gun so please don't do anything stupid."

"All right," I said meekly.

She produced a key. I held up my wrist and she unlocked the cuff, then held open the dressing gown. I hesitated a moment, then turned and put my arms into the sleeves. She folded it over my shoulders. I quickly stepped away and did up the sash. She moved to the door and opened it. Cal was still standing on the landing.

"This way."

I followed her down the passage and she indicated for me to

go through a door on the right. I glanced at Cal, at the landing he was on and the flight of stairs that ran down from it.

"Into the bathroom please, Miss Farewell," Dr Kent said crisply. "You can have twenty minutes. Calvin and I will be out here."

The bathroom was rather cramped under the pitched roof, but contained bath, washbasin and loo. The light was on and the Velux window was shuttered like the one in the bedroom. It was possible to shut the door, but not to lock it. A bath had already been run.

The first thing I did was to brush my teeth to try and get rid of the bad taste that still lingered in my mouth. Then, with a look at the door, I undressed and stepped into the bath. I washed, then added some more hot water and lay back. Some sort of bath oil had been added and the aroma and the warmth of the water seemed to soak into me, relax me. My mind became calm, almost detached.

If she has released Tom, I thought, and somehow I did believe her, then surely it's only a matter of time before he and Marcus find me. Perhaps it might be better just to sit tight and not make any trouble.

A tap on the door cut through my reverie.

"Could you come out now, please, Miss Farewell?"

"I'm just getting out of the bath."

"Two minutes."

I clambered out. As I reached for the towel, which was beside the washbasin, a draught chilled my legs. It seemed to be coming from a grill formed of wooden slats in the wall that was adjacent to the basin. I stretched a hand towards it and felt the air cooling my fingers. Some sort of air-conditioning?

"One more minute, Miss Farewell."

I snatched the towel, hurriedly dried myself and struggled into nightdress and dressing gown.

"I'm ready."

The door opened.

Dr Kent said. "Back in the bedroom, please."

She followed me. I could sense Cal watching us. Inside, she picked up the cuff and threaded it into the wire loop again. "Hold out your wrist, please."

"Is it really necessary?"

"For the moment. I'm afraid it is."

I held out my wrist and she snapped it round. Then, she gently pushed the door closed.

"Do you feel better for your bath?"

"Thank you, yes."

"Good. Sit down, please." She indicated the bed, taking the armchair herself. She gazed at me a moment. "We mean you no harm, Miss Farewell. If you co-operate, nothing bad is going to happen to you."

"Why am I here?"

"You have videos, CDs and books. Within reason, I will try and get you anything you want."

"Why am I here, Dr Kent?"

"Meanwhile, be patient and we will try to make you as comfortable as possible."

Perhaps I'd pushed that enough for now. I said, "What about exercise? Can I go outside?"

"There's an exercise bike downstairs. I'll bring it up if you like."

"All right," I said.

"If you need someone," she began slowly, but another thought had occurred to me . . .

"What if I need the loo?"

"You can use the bathroom twice a day, morning and evening. Otherwise, use the chamber pot."

I was regretting having used it earlier now – a precedent had been set.

"What I if need to . . . to pass a motion?"

She stared at me in silence for a moment. "Try to do so in the morning or evening. If it's really urgent . . ." she hesitated . . . "I'll make an exception. Do you need to go now?"

I shook my head.

"As I was about to say," she continued. "If you feel the need to talk to someone, I'll spend time with you. Otherwise, I'll leave you alone."

"Dr Kent" – I leant forward, unable to help myself, pleading with my eyes – "please, tell me why I'm here."

She stood up. "I'll bring the exercise bike up after lunch." She moved quickly across the room and let herself out. The lock rattled and the bolt was pushed home.

She can do that, I thought. Go whenever she feels like it. Just like that. A surge of anger took me, so acute it made me tremble.

Twenty-Two

Keep hold of the anger, another part of me told myself, use it. Imagine Tom's here – what would he do?

Well, in the first palce, he'd know what to do about this bloody cuff. I lifted my hand, peered at it and tried to push a finger between it and my wrist. It wouldn't go, in fact the coated wire was slightly uncomfortable where it pressed into my wrist and I didn't even try forcing the cuff over my hand. The plastic the cuff was made of was strong and I doubted even a sharp knife would cut into it – it would need a hacksaw.

I sighed and looked more closely at the coated wire. It was about a quarter of an inch thick altogether. A really sharp knife might make some impression – given time. Well, I had plenty of that, shame about the knife.

I followed the wire over to the radiator where it was hitched round the copper pipe and tugged experimentally – both radiator and pipe seemed solidly attached. Even if I could free myself, how would I get past the door and Cal?

A wave a lethargy swept over me, I sank back on to my heels and thought: I really can't be bothered with all this now. I think I knew I was being sedated, but I didn't care about that, either.

You've got it cushy, Jo. I thought, compared with Terry Waite and those others in Beirut. Dr Kent isn't going to harm you, and there's a chance, every chance that Tom and Marcus will find you.

After a while, I pushed myself up and went over to the CDs and shuffled through them. I chose Mozart's Fortieth because

I didn't understand how anyone could write forty symphonies, put it in the CD player and lay on the bed.

Diddle dee, diddle dee, diddle dee dee – the music washed over me, into me, through me. It's a sad piece of music, sad, and angry too. I'd never realised that before. When it was finished, I thought about it for a while, then played it again. I was still lying on the bed thinking when the door opened and Dr Kent came in.

"Lunch, Miss Farewell," she said, and I realised I had no conception whatever of the passage of time. I thanked her and she left.

Lunch was tuna mixed with rice and a salad. I was still hungry and ate it all, followed by more coffee. I didn't care if it was drugged. Lemon meringue pie for pudding.

She brought the exercise bike up when she came for the tray and after she'd gone, I tried it out. Not for long though, too tiring.

I switched on the TV and fed *Hannah and her Sisters* into the video player (neither the TV nor radio worked, which didn't surprise me). I became quietly absorbed and, after it was finished, I thought: Strange, for all his mucky private life, Woody Allen does understand women. Lying on my bed, staring up at the pitched ceiling, I thought about this, and then about Tom. He doesn't understand women, I thought, or does he? So insensitive sometimes, selfish, crude almost, and yet . . . sensual.

Would he understand Dr Kent enough to find me?

Dinner. Some sort of beef casserole, quite tasty. Dr Kent was her friendly, reserved, polite self. Afterwards, I looked through the books. There were Margaret Drabble, Jeanette Winterson, Edna O'Brien, Fay Weldon.

As a kind of protest, I pulled out a battered copy of *Tess of the D'Urbervilles* and to my surprise, became immersed in the descriptions of Wessex, of a young country girl's life and dreams. They were so different from mine, although it had only been written a hundred years before and when Dr Kent came to take me to the bathroom, it was almost an interruption.

On the loo, to my irritation, I ran out of paper. There was an unopened pack of rolls on the floor beside me, between the pan and the bath and I reached down for it. Underneath, beside the wood panelling of the bath, something glinted. I reached down again. Whatever it was, was jammed underneath the panelling. I tried to get a fingernail behind it.

"Are you ready, Miss Farewell?"

"I'm on the loo," I shouted.

Was it worth it? I probed with my nail one more time and out slid a nail file which I quickly slipped into my dressing-gown pocket.

Later, in bed, I thought: No way would it get through the cuff, but what about the wire? I'd left it in the dressing gown, which was hanging on the back of the door.

I slept without too much difficulty, probably because of the sedatives, and dreamt that I was back in Latchvale and that it was Dr Kent, the clinic and my prison that were a dream. When I woke, I couldn't understand why the cuff was still there and the moment of realisation was awful. I wanted to scream, but something stopped me. I had to cry though, and wept into my pillow again. It was a relief when the door gave its familiar rattle and Dr Kent came in.

I stopped crying, but lay with my head still buried in the pillow.

"Are you all right, Miss Farewell? What's the matter?"

My head came up in a flash. "What d'you bloody think is the matter?"

"I've brought you some coffee."

"I don't want it."

"I'll leave it on the table."

"It's drugged, isn't it?"

"I've added a mild sedative, yes. In the circumstances, it can only help you."

"Letting me go would be even more help."

"I'm afraid that's not possible at the moment. I'd like to examine you now, please."

I thought very hard about resisting, but the prospect of being manhandled by Cal was too much.

"I want to use the loo first," I said, by way of token resistance.

"I'd be grateful if you could hang on for a few moments," she said. "A full bladder's better for the scan."

It was the 'I'd be grateful' that really banged it home to me just how impotent I was. I submitted, but my throat swelled and my eyes pricked and tears trickled down my face again. And again, a look of genuine compassion filled her own eyes for a moment.

"I really will try to be quick," she said, although we both knew that wasn't the reason I was crying.

After she'd taken my blood pressure and temperature, she brought the scanner in again, applied gel and studied the screen as she moved the sensor over my abdomen.

"Dr Kent—"

"Please don't talk while I'm doing this." Her face was totally absorbed by the screen. It was her very absorption that had made me speak.

"I beg you, please tell me what you're doing to me."

Her head came up and she snapped. "Will you *please* let me do this."

The suddenness shocked me and I didn't say any more.

After she'd gone, I used the chamber pot, then drank the coffee she'd left. I did so out of helplessness. It did seem to make me feel slightly better. I didn't eat much breakfast, perhaps because I had eaten so much the day before. In the bath, the feeling of detachment, of being able to observe myself stole over me again, but a dull misery was all there was to see.

Back in my room, I tried some Beethoven, but it seemed an irrelevance. I lay on my bed, got up again, paced the room. I couldn't face the thought of a video and *Tess* just didn't hold me the way it had yesterday.

I tried to remember what I'd read about prisoners like Terry Waite. They'd kept themselves thinking, about the tiny things going on around them, about what they'd do when they were free, about *anything*.

But there was nothing going on around me, except a blackbird singing somewhere outside. I tried to concentrate on it, but it must have flown away. Or had I imagined it?

What would I do when I was free? A binge? A holiday with my mother?

Perhaps. But what I wanted most of all was just to walk the streets of Latchvale again being me, Jo Farewell, with no pretences, no stratagems. Shops, some new clothes, a hair-do . . . and then to hear the solid snick of my own front door closing behind me when I got home. When I got . . . !

The fuzziness in my head became a jangle, expanding, overflowing, surging along my nerves until my joints, my very fingertips seemed to scream with static electricity. I jumped up, strode over to the exercise bike and pedalled furiously for as long as I could, which wasn't very long, then lay on my bed again, panting.

Music; Mozart's Fortieth again, turned right up until my eardrums hurt in an effort to drown everything else out. Diddle dee, diddle dee, diddle dee dee . . . I didn't hear the door, just became aware of Kent's presence as she walked across the room and turned the music down.

"Would you like some lunch?" she asked.

"No thank you."

"Not hungry?"

"No."

"You didn't eat much breakfast."

"No."

She regarded me thoughtfully.

"Would you like to talk?"

"What about?"

"Anything you like."

"There's only one thing I want to talk to you about."

176

"We could talk about you, your life. We could talk about Mr Jones, if you like."

I didn't say anything. The music played softly.

"You're fond of him, aren't you?" she said.

"It's a professional relationship."

"He may be that kind of professional, but you aren't. Is he married?"

"Yes. And he has a son," I added defiantly.

She smiled quickly. "He had me completely fooled, you know. I've seen plenty of infertile men and I could have sworn he had all the hallmarks."

"As you said, he's a professional."

"I could also see that you were genuinely fond of him, although I couldn't understand why at the time."

"You can now?"

"Oh yes, he's a very clever and resourceful man. Does his wife know how you feel?"

"I – I think so, but she's—"

"She's—?" Dr Kent prompted.

I realised she'd drawn me into talking to her and how much I needed to talk to someone. Did it matter if I talked to her?

"She knows he'd never leave her now they have a son."

"Would he have before?"

"I . . . don't know."

"Would you want him to?"

"I don't know that either."

"If he were to, it wouldn't work, you know."

"No, probably not," I agreed.

She considered me a moment. "How did you meet him?"

"Does it matter?"

"Not really."

"You didn't like him, did you, Dr Kent?"

"Not very much, no."

I swallowed. "He probably saved my life."

"I wondered if it was something like that," she said softly.

"It's not hero worship or anything like that," I said quickly.

177

"I didn't think it was," she said equably. She would have made a good counsellor because I found myself telling her about the serial killer in Latchvale hospital and how Tom had become involved, while the other part of me wondered whether she'd slipped some sort of truth drug in with the sedative.

You're playing her game, this other part of me warned. I couldn't see how.

"He seems a rather ruthless young man," she said when I'd finished. "But I can understand why you found him attractive."

"How d'you mean, ruthless?"

"He deliberately put you at risk. Used you, in fact."

"He had no choice, not if he was to find the killer."

My other self smiled sardonically: *That's not what you said at the time.* At the time I'd hated him for it.

"So the end justified the means?" Dr Kent said.

"Ye-es. No, it wasn't like that."

She shrugged. "Perhaps not."

"You don't like men, do you, Dr Kent?" I said in an effort to take the initiative from her.

"Certainly there are a great many men I don't like. You do like them, I take it?"

"Yes, but that wasn't what I meant. I meant males, maleness, not just numbers of men."

"The great majority of men use women," she said, "and that's why I don't like the great majority of them."

"It works both ways, surely?"

"We're all equal now, you mean?" She leant forward. "Because we're in what some men are pleased to call the post-feminist era. That, my dear, is a confidence trick. Men still rule the roost."

"But we've had a woman prime minister for God's sake!"

"Yes. But the few women who do make it to the top do so by being like those men, aping them, dancing to their tune."

"I don't understand."

She swallowed and took a breath. "Our political system, our

industrial system, our very family life has been evolved by the male, for the male. So those women who do succeed have to pretend to be men. Women won't, cannot be fulfilled until they have altered these basic systems to reflect female interests."

"I simply don't understand what you mean, Dr Kent."

"No, perhaps not," she said, sinking back. "Try looking at it in another way. Look at the men in your life, look at them and their careers, look hard and honestly and then tell me that they didn't use you. Do it now if you like."

"I can't, not on the spur of the moment."

"I expect you are already."

She was right, I was . . . Alan, whom I'd thought I'd marry one day. We'd been together nearly two years. Oh, he'd cried when he ended it, I could see his eyes glistening now, but he'd still left me for another woman – a doctor, like him. Whom he'd married.

And then there was Stephen . . .

"It works both ways," I said firmly.

"Your expression belies your words," she said. "And yet you'd still get married, wouldn't you?"

"Yes, to the right man." As soon as the words came out. I could have bitten my tongue.

She smiled. "Mr Right, in fact?"

"Have you ever been married, Dr Kent?" I demanded harshly. "Have you ever had a sexual relationship with a man?"

Her face froze. "Yes."

Her eyes slewed away from me as the most terrifying bleakness flooded her face. I was too shocked to say anything more and after a moment, her face composed once more, she got up from the chair.

"I'll bring you your lunch," she said, and quickly left the room.

Twenty-Three

W hat on earth could have made her react like that?
Failed marriage? No. Failed relationship? Was she,
in Tom's delicate phraseology, nothing but a suppressed dyke?
No, I somehow didn't think so.

Might that not be wishful thinking? my other self observed
wryly. At times like this, my other self seemed to take on a
personality of its own, like an evil little sprite or homunculus
inside me.

No, my impression of her being sexless, like the *Walking
Madonna*, was probably nearer the truth.

Rape, then? Much more likely – women who have been
raped never feel quite the same about men again.

At this moment, she came back in, holding a tray.

"Your lunch."

"Thank you."

I studied her covertly as she put the tray on the table. Her
face was devoid of any expression, although her eyes had
briefly met mine when she spoke. Her body seemed relaxed
– it was as though our conversation hadn't taken place. It was
iron self-control. She left the room silently.

Curiously, our talk had left me feeling better and I ate most
of my lunch (pizza and salad) thinking as I did about the things
she'd said.

Were women used by men generally? Most top jobs were
held by men (although not in nursing!), but was this due to
women being used? Perhaps, in that woman often subsumed
their ambition in motherhood, but to an extent, that was a

matter of choice. Was this what she was getting at – better facilities for mothers in top jobs? An image flickered of a lady MP getting to her feet to speak in the House of Commons with a baby clamped to her breast. No, she had meant more than that. There *was* a division between the sexes in certain jobs: nursing, for instance, mostly female; the army, mostly male; politics, ditto. Was this what she'd been getting at?

As though on cue, she came in to collect the tray.

"Ah, your appetite's returned." She studied me briefly as though wanting to know why. "I'm glad about that."

After she'd gone, I found myself thinking about the men in my life again, there had been others besides Alan and Stephen.

Had they used me?

No: at least not sexually, that would have been mutual. Wouldn't it?

Looking back, it did seem to me that they'd all, at least subconsciously, assumed that their careers were more important than mine, even when the relationship hadn't been that serious. Or was I imagining it? Was Dr Kent getting to me?

I gave it up and went over to the exercise bike. This time, I took it slowly, emptying my mind of everything except the stretching of the muscles in my legs and feet, and when at last I'd had enough, I lay on my back on the bed, feeling my whole body relax. The blackbird outside was singing again.

Later, I watched *Educating Rita* and after she'd cleared away dinner (turkey escalopes), Dr Kent surprised me by suggesting a game of chess. She'd noticed Tom and me playing, she said. I thought it best to agree.

I've heard it said that men play chess deliberately, whereas women play by intuition. I wouldn't know about that, but every move she made was with the utmost deliberation and I soon realised that I had absolutely no chance of beating her. After two games, I told her there wasn't much point in continuing.

She said, "Well, it wouldn't have done for me to have patronised you by allowing you to win, would it?"

"Of course not," I said awkwardly, wondering at the clumsy way she expressed herself sometimes. I added, "It would have been interesting to see you and Tom play."

"Is he good?"

"He always beats me. Well, usually."

"A lot of it's psychology, you know." She leant back, looking at me steadily. "Which of us d'you think would win?"

"Oh, you would."

"Why?"

"Because you're . . . you're more patient, more self-contained."

Her eyes were still, grey pools. She said. "You must have wondered why I reacted the way I did earlier."

"It's not really any of my—"

"I'm going to tell you."

You're not going like it, my sprite, my homunculus warned.

"When I was a child, Catcott Manor was my home, I grew up there in the forties and fifties. I see from your expression that you were already aware of that."

I cleared my throat. "Yes. Tom and his boss – er – looked into your background."

"Did they?" Her voice didn't express much interest. "There were complications at my birth and I was an only child. Nevertheless, I had a happy enough childhood until I was ten, when my mother died." She drew in a breath then released it. "Daddy was very kind and said that we were all we had left now, and that we had to look after each other. Comfort each other. He took me to his bed with him. At first, I thought it was a new kind of game and by the time I realised what he was doing to me, it was too late. Too late."

I suppose I'd been expecting something of the kind, but I still felt sick. "I'm terribly sorry, Dr Kent. But—"

"All I could do was to endure and work hard at school so that I could become qualified and escape."

"But couldn't you have reported him?"

"This was the fifties, Miss Farewell, and child abuse hadn't" been invented. Besides, Daddy was the local squire, a pillar of the community."

"But couldn't you have told someone at school, one of your teachers?"

"I did. They went to my father who told them that I was over-imaginative and neurotic. He beat me as soon as they'd gone."

"Didn't anyone notice?"

"He beat me on the body where it didn't show, and put the fear of Satan into me so that I never said another word to anyone."

I touched my lips with the tip of my tongue. "Weren't there any relatives you could have spoken to?"

"There was only his sister, my aunt. She was fond of me, but this would have been outside her imagination. She'd have assumed I was mad, or evil. But my aunt did have her uses." The tiniest smile touched her lips. "When I was a bit older, I told her I wanted to become a doctor, but that my father was against it. She had no trouble in believing that, and was able to coerce him into letting me try. Daddy tried to sabotage my studies, of course, but with my aunt's help, I made it."

"So you did manage to escape." It sounded fatuous as I said it, but it was all I could think of to say.

"Obviously." Her eyes never left my face.

"I'm appalled by your story, Dr Kent. But why have you told me?"

"Because I wanted you to know. Besides, you must have realised something of the kind after this afternoon."

"I . . . realised there had to be a reason for your hatred of men."

"It's not that I hate men, Miss Farewell, I merely understand them. My experiences have made me aware of how all of them have this same congenital flaw, this absolute need to dominate women."

"You really think all men are like that?"

Her eyes gleamed. "I know all men are like that."

"But what about the women who abuse boys?"

"You will find, invariably, that such women have themselves been abused by a man, usually their father. So it is merely another form of male abuse."

She was mad, although I could understand why. I said carefully, "I don't think my own father was like that."

"Were your parents happily married?"

"Yes, they were."

"And your father died first?"

"Yes."

She nodded. "Marriage is the device whereby the worst of male impulses are kept in check. It has evolved over the centuries for that purpose. But as soon as the marriage breaks down, or the influence of the mother is removed in some other way, then the male will revert."

There was another silence.

"I can't believe they *all* revert," I said.

Careful, Jo, warned homunculus, *she's a fruitcake.*

It needn't have worried, she continued as though I hadn't spoken.

"That's why I believe." she said, "that the time has come for women to find a completely new basis for their relationship with men. One genuinely based on equality."

"Dr Kent. what have you been doing to me?" I couldn't stop myself. "Why am I here. You *must* tell me."

"You must trust me."

As I looked back at her, I found myself actually wanting to. I said, "I don't think I can bear much more of this."

"I'm going to leave you with some sleeping pills tonight, in case you can't sleep."

"I don't want any more drugs."

"I'll leave them with you anyway. It will be your choice."

I couldn't sleep. Every time I closed my eyes, new thoughts, new possibilities grew behind them. What had she been doing – above all to me?

My worst fear was that she'd replaced eggs in me. But she'd told me the day before she hadn't and I'd believed her.

I had the impression that she always told the truth where possible. And even if she had implanted eggs, why did she keep scanning me? It takes at least two weeks before pregnancy can be confirmed, either by scanning or urine analysis, and I simply hadn't been here long enough.

Can you be sure of that? asked homunculus.

Not sure, no, but I didn't think so.

Was she planning to replace eggs at a later date?

Whatever it was, she was clearly insane and I hoped desperately that Tom and Marcus would find me soon.

But would they? Yes, because it's virtually impossible to hide in this country for any length of time, there are too many nosy people. But are you still in this country?

I realised that I could be anywhere . . . *anywhere.*

I took the sleeping pills and tried to read more of *Tess* while I waited for them to work.

I didn't waken until she came to examine and scan me the next morning. I was uncomfortable, still half asleep, and wished she'd just go away. As soon as she had gone, I used the chamber pot and drank the coffee, and ached for a cigarette.

Breakfast didn't appeal and even the bath left me feeling scratchy and irritable. Back in my room, the day stretched drearily ahead and I was at a complete loss to know what to do when the key rattled and she came in.

"Come and sit down, Miss Farewell." There was something different about her. Yesterday, she'd been unsure of herself at times, veering between diffidence and certainty; now her self-confidence overflowed, she was almost – triumphant.

"I'm going to complete the story I began telling you yesterday."

Twenty-Four

A re you sitting comfortably? homunculus drolly enquired. "With my aunt's help," Dr Kent began, "I escaped to medical school in Liverpool, where I devoted myself to my studies and tried to forget the past. I qualified as a doctor in the early sixties and specialised in obstetrics and gynaecology. As part of my fellowship training. I worked for a period in a community clinic where I saw things that brought my past back all too clearly." Her voice became slower, her eyes faraway. "Women beaten in the final stages of pregnancy because they didn't want sexual intercourse. Women with prolapses brought about by the way they were forced to work before and after childbirth. Women enduring hell from violent, drunken husbands. Women used up before they were thirty."

"It's not like that any more," I said feebly.

"Oh, where have *you* been living for goodness' sake?" she snapped. "Ah, yes," she said with a little smile, "Latchvale. Middle England, middle class." The smile faded and she continued, more quickly, "I thought at first that education and contraception were the answers, and to that end, started a self-help group for women in that position. It was a success and we did some very good work, but after a while, I found myself dissatisfied and wanting to make a more significant contribution. Self-help groups, useful though they are, are merely palliatives. I had to do something to change the basic attitudes that have perpetuated the subjugation of women. To do this, I had to become a consultant." She sighed. "This took time and a great deal of effort, but eventually,

I succeeded. Once established, I began to make changes in the way obstetrics was practised to make it . . . more user friendly, shall we say? My male colleagues took a dim view of this and began trying to discredit my methods and undermine my position. Then, one of my patients unfortunately died, a case was trumped up against me and I was suspended pending enquiry."

"What did she die of?" I asked.

"Eclampsia. The enquiry mostly absolved me" (mostly?) "but I was told privately that there was no future for me in that hospital. As a sop, I was offered a job in another hospital, at the newly created fertility clinic." She smiled, reminiscently. "Curiously, this was perhaps the happiest period of my life. I became an acknowledged expert in fertility techniques and, although I wasn't directly involved, no one cheered louder than me when Louise Brown was born in 1978."

Fleetingly, I remembered Professor Fulbourn's reference to this, about a hundred years earlier.

"Then, in 1982, I was approached by a homosexual woman who was desperate for a baby, but for whom the thought of sexual intercourse was anathema. After interviewing her, I saw no reason why she shouldn't make an excellent parent and arranged for her to have donor insemination. Others followed. Homosexual women with blocked tubes were referred to me and I arranged for them to have IVF. Then, one of the homosexual women I had helped was charged with abusing and killing her son. It transpired that she had a rare form of schizophrenia, undetectable when I interviewed her, which led to the tragedy. Once again, the Male Medical Mafia struck, and I was suspended pending enquiry. I took sabbatical leave and went to America, to stay with Carla Goldberg, whom I already knew slightly. She was at that time a researcher at a fertility clinic in Baltimore. We discovered that we had a great deal in common."

She paused and studied me for a moment. When she began speaking again, it was as though she was delivering a lecture, an incantation, something she'd gone over time and again.

"It has become almost a cliché that men cause all the misery and suffering in the world through their ridiculous need to compete and the violence that springs from it, while women have to endure and repair; but clichés tend to become clichés because they are apposite."

"I thought that men competed in order for the species to evolve." I felt I had to keep up a presence in order not to be swamped by her.

"Now that we have a stable environment, that function is redundant." She leant forward. "Throughout recorded history, the Genesis theory has been accepted and it has been assumed that women are an offshoot of man, merely the means by which he reproduces himself. Men have been able to impose this spurious philosophy through their superior size and strength, and their willingness to use them." She took a breath and released it. "Science and logic have now turned this theory on its head. Science has proved that in terms of the multi-celled animal, it the *female* form that is the basic form, and the male which is an offshoot, evolved solely for the purpose of genetic variability. This perhaps goes some way to explaining why women live longer than men and are less prone to genetic disorders."

"You could well be right, Dr Kent," I said. "But what possible relevance does it have for human beings today?"

"*Every* relevance. It is the female who provides the *matériel* for existence, the ovum, the womb, the sustenance. The male is a parasite on the female; all he provides is a half-complement of genes."

"Isn't that rather an essential 'all'?"

"Men cannot possibly reproduce without women. Women, in theory at least, *can* reproduce without men."

There was a silence and I felt suddenly very tired.

"Is this some kind of weird plot to get rid of men, Dr Kent?"

"No. I don't wish to harm men in any way. All I wish is to give women the choice as to whether or not they allow men into their lives."

"Surely, that choice already exists."

"It does not and will not until women have the power, the *right*, to procreate without men. Then and only then will they be able to make that choice."

I had already seen where this was leading and was sick to my soul. I tried to keep my voice steady. "It's not possible. It's been tried with animals and it hasn't worked."

"On the contrary, it *is* possible. Frogs and toads were successfully cloned a long time ago, and more recently, so have sheep."

"I don't believe you."

"Not only is it *possible*, Miss Farewell," she bit off the words, poking her head at me, "but it happened in nature long before it was ever brought about in the laboratory." She took another deep breath and moderated her tone. "Some creatures, a fish known as the Amazon Molly, for instance, have dispensed with the male altogether and reverted to asexuality, to cloning if you like, because their environment has become stable and there is no longer any need for biological variety. The same applies to the rest of life – we go on using sex out of biological habit. We are trapped by it."

"Some creatures may have changed genetically in nature," I said, trying to keep my voice steady, "but to bring it about in the laboratory is not right, not natural."

"The very fact that we are here at all is not natural. Humans have used genetic manipulation ever since they discovered the mutant strains of grass we now call wheat. We rely on technology to feed, clothe and keep ourselves alive, so why should we not use it to enhance ourselves?"

"Because it's not *natural*," my voice rose to a squeak. "If you push nature too hard, it hits back."

"Really? Well, it seems to me that we've pushed nature a long way already and we're five billion and growing."

"Just what have you been doing, Dr Kent?" I demanded.

"I will tell you. Carla and I quickly discovered that we had been thinking along the same lines and we formed a group whose aim was to enable women to reproduce without men. Carla had already done some clandestine research, but had realised she needed a much larger pool of subjects, the size of pool coming to a fertility clinic, for instance. Although Carla did have some money of her own, it wasn't enough for us to start our own clinic, so we contented ourselves with experiments in the laboratory, and on eggs from each other.

"Then my father died. He had sold Catcott Manor to National Heritage and then leased it back for a period to cover his lifetime. I inherited all his money and the remaining five years of the lease. National Heritage wanted to buy me out, and I was about to sell when it occurred to us that it was just the sort of site we needed. It was also a form of poetic justice. It took us nearly a year to set it up, equip it and pass inspection. We decided we would experiment on suitable patients once only before using conventional treatment for the next cycle. Carla had already performed experiments stimulating the human ovum to start replicating on its own without any sperm, so this is what we did first."

"Stimulated DNA," I breathed.

"As you say. These experiments ultimately didn't work. We grew viable embryos *in vitro* to the four-cell stage and replaced them. They would embed in the womb and grow, but there were problems with the forming of the placenta which led to early spontaneous abortion. We were not entirely surprised, and had besides always been aware of the dangers of a diminishing gene pool, which would have led eventually to recessive gene disorders."

"How many women did you do this to?" I asked in a hushed voice.

"About twenty."

"And they never realised?"

"No. Many of them became pregnant in a later cycle

of conventional treatment, so they had nothing to complain about."

"That's *outrageous*—" I began, but she overrode me.

"By this time, we had our first microinjection equipment, so we tried cloning proper. We would take an unfertilised egg, remove the haploid nucleus, which contains only half the human complement of chromosomes and replace it with the nucleus from a diploid cell, which contains the full complement of forty-six chromosomes."

"Replaced DNA. Did it work?"

"Yes, eventually, although only if egg and nucleus came from the same person and were replaced in that person."

"So you're saying that a cloned human being is actually in existence?"

"Not as yet, although the mother is pregnant. And you needn't say it so reprovingly. An identical twin is a cloned human being, and we don't regard them as freaks."

"But they occur *naturally*."

"When it became obvious that we could make this work, we moved on to our third project."

The words Nuclear DNA flashed in my brain, but I was past speaking. I stared at her in sick fascination.

"There is nothing remarkable or magic about the male set of haploid chromosomes other than the possession of the y chromosome, which codes for another male in approximately half the sets. There is no reason why a haploid set from one female egg should not integrate with the haploid set from another thus also ensuring genetic variability. The only difference would be that all the resulting offspring would be female. The problem was getting the two haploid sets to integrate. Whole nuclei didn't work, so we had to disrupt the nuclear membrane of the donor nucleus before injecting it into the recipient, not easy, even with an operator as skilled as Chrystal. I won't go into all the experimental detail, but we did eventually succeed in getting the nuclei to fuse and form an embryo."

She seemed now to be staring past my shoulder, as though telling the story to someone behind me.

"We then tried implanting the embryos at different stages of development, but none of them grew *in vitro*."

I relaxed a little at this, although it was obvious they were going to try some kind of experiment on me.

"Why me?" I asked.

She started slightly as though becoming aware of my existence again. "Because we then tried a novel procedure. Nobody can be sure why the GIFT procedure, placing egg and sperm together in the Fallopian tube, should work any better than placing an embryo in the womb, but sometimes it does. So we tried the same with freshly microinjected eggs, replacing them in the tubes in the same operation. It has achieved one pregnancy, a pregnancy that went to three months."

"Denny," I whispered . . .

"Indeed, which is why we broke our rule with her, and tried again."

"Is that what you've done to me?"

"Yes. We replaced six DNA microinjected eggs in your tubes, within two hours of taking them from your ovaries."

"It won't work . . . it *can't* work . . ."

"It *has* worked."

"You can't possibly know that." I found a straw and clung to it. "It takes at least two weeks to confirm. You can't possibly—"

"You're forgetting the Colour Flow Doppler scanning equipment you showed such an interest in at the clinic. Last Wednesday, at the manor, I detected two poly-celled embryos in your tubes. One of these has embedded in your womb and has now formed its own blood supply. You're pregnant, Miss Farewell, a pregnancy that will make history. With DNA from an egg donated by me."

Twenty-Five

S*he's put you in the family way* . . . homunculus said, and watched as I launched myself at her.

I caught her completely by surprise, the look of astonishment on her face would have been comical in any other situation. She just had time for one gurgle before my thumbs pressed into her windpipe and I felt a surge of primeval joy. I was going to kill her.

Her hands fumbled at my wrists, then, with surprising speed, her fingers jabbed into my eyes and my own hands flew up to them.

"Calvin!" she screeched, "Calvin!"

We struggled, then Cal's fingers dug into my upper arms, paralysing them. I let go and was lifted bodily away from her. I shouted, screamed, struggled – God, he was strong.

"Shuddup," he said in my ear, "or I'll really hurt you." His breath stank of garlic. I let myself go limp.

Dr Kent was dark-faced and coughing. She struggled out of the chair.

"That was a very stupid thing to do." Her voice came out as a croak.

I shouted at her, "If I can't kill you, then I'll kill myself."

"You will not."

"You've raped me," I screamed. "You're no better than your father."

She smacked the side of my face with all her might. I would have collapsed but for Cal holding me up.

I raised my head and looked at her but didn't say anything.

My cheek stung abominably and I knew if I said another word, she'd hit me again. She stared back, challenging me.

At last she said. "Do you want sedation?" It was a serious question. Her voice wasn't so croaky now.

"No." I gulped. "I just want to left alone."

To my surprise, she said, "Yes, that might be best for now." She cleared her throat. "I meant what I said earlier, I mean you no harm. Whatever the outcome, if you co-operate, you'll be released afterwards, if that's what you want. D'you understand?"

I nodded dumbly.

"Let her go, Calvin."

I swayed, but remained upright.

"Within reason. I'll discuss any aspect with you, help you in any way I can, provided you co-operate."

"Can I sit down?"

"Of course."

I sat down on the side of the bed.

"I'll leave you now, although I shall look in at intervals to make sure you don't try anything stupid." She glanced round the room. "Not that you have much scope here." She cleared her throat again. "Try to come to terms with this. I'm available if you need to talk. All right?"

"All right." I just wanted her to go.

Cal opened the door for her and she went out without looking back. As soon as the door shut, I was on my knees heaving up what breakfast I'd had into the chamber pot.

It was funny, but this other part of me, this vile homunculus, went on watching and commenting, no matter how bad things got.

Morning sickness? it said now.

I rinsed my mouth out and sat on the bed again. Was there any chance she could be wrong?

No, said homunculus. *No, she knows her stuff, even if she is seriously mad.*

I began to cry, softly at first, then with more intensity into the familiar pillow. Homunculus watched. No one came in. I thought, I'm pregnant – *pregnant* – with a monster.

Could I kill myself?

No, you won't do that.

No, I won't, I agreed, although I was still crying. Not yet, anyway – Tom and Marcus could find me at any time.

I wouldn't rely on that, if I were you. She's confident of holding you for another nine months, she must have a reason for that.

I was still crying as this conversation with myself went on, my body jerking spasmodically. The blackbird was singing again. It sounded as though it were bursting with joy and its sheer freedom made me think about killing myself again.

No, don't do that. You'd only regret it later.

Ha, ha.

Think about the blackbird.

I thought about the blackbird. Its notes were a sort of rich purple-yellow, almost painful, coming out of the wall beside me.

Why?

Still snivelling, I turned on my side and stared at the wall. I reached over and touched the wallpaper. It gave slightly under my fingers, there were a series of ridges, or slats underneath, rather like the grill in the bathroom.

I stared at the wall, at the pitched ceiling above, then back at the wall again. *There's a space behind it running all the way round the room.* No, not all the way round, I thought, only on the three sides where the ceiling's pitched.

I tapped the wall next to the grill – hollow – and worked it out. I'd thought it was an attic, but it was more likely to be a loft conversion. I remembered a friend who'd had one done, and the space behind the walls.

Grill? It was a door, so that the space could be used for storage or access.

The lock rattled and I twisted round. Dr Kent came in and I turned away, scared she would read my mind.

"I'll clear this up for you," she said, picking up the chamber pot. "Is there anything else you need?"

I shook my head slowly, not looking at her. She went out. I heard her clean the chamber pot in the bathroom. She brought it back in, replaced it and went out again.

Did she know about the grill? Had she papered it over herself?

I examined the wallpaper. No, there was no giveaway demarcation line.

All right, I thought, so there *may* be a way past the locked door, but what about this? I held my wrist up with Tom's cuff and the plastic-covered wire.

What about the nail file? Steady, Jo.

My mind was on fire. The file might get through the plastic, but would it get through the wire inside?

It's got a point, hasn't it? For cleaning your nails. Push that under each strand and file 'em through one at a time.

But would it, *could* it work?

Can't hurt to try, can it?

When? Tonight?

It was so tempting. I just wanted to be gone. But it needed thinking out. Would the door into the space open? I had to have a good look at the one in the bathroom, perhaps I could do that this evening.

I took the nail file out of my dressing-gown pocket – it would be just my luck for Dr Kent to put her hand in now. It looked so puny . . . *could* it get through the wire?

I tried filing at the plastic coating. It was tough, but the file did make an impression. Maybe I should start at the radiator and where no one would notice. I could even start now – no, Dr Kent might come in at any time. I quickly hid the file under the music centre.

It was tempting, too, to pull the bed away from the wall and have a better look at the grill, but the same argument applied.

What kind of surface would there be in there? Rafters, probably. OK so long as I didn't put any weight between them. I paced the distance I'd have to crawl – would there be any obstructions? Maybe not if one of the functions was access – but what about the corner? There was no way of knowing till I got there. I tried to imagine the bathroom beyond the wall. It was small, a couple of paces at most.

The door opened and Dr Kent came in with a tray. "Your lunch."

"I don't want any." Still the fear that she would somehow read my mind.

"I'll leave it here anyway."

After she'd gone. I tried moving the bed. It was heavy, but it did move. I didn't have any lunch or any coffee.

"No appetite, Miss Farewell?" she said when she came for the tray.

"No."

"And you haven't touched your coffee."

"You know why."

"Mild sedation can only help you at the moment. Would you prefer tea?"

I pretended to consider this. "All right."

She left me alone for most of the afternoon and I spent the time thinking, planning . . .

Would the bathroom grill open?

Check it tonight – ask her if you can have a bath to give you more time.

But won't she wonder why I want a bath?

Tell her you've got vomit on yourself.

If I filed through the wire at the radiator end, I'd have to drag the rest of it round with me, but if I did it at the cuff end and couldn't get through it in one night, she'd notice.

The afternoon dragged, but not as much as it might – my mind was too full. I worked my way through several symphonies while I planned. Mozart seemed to stimulate thought more than Beethoven.

What do I do if I make it? No, *when* I make it to the bathroom? Try and overpower them in their sleep?

Don't be stupid!
Look for the phone?
No, just get out and look for a call-box, phone for help.
What if I was in another country?
The same – look for a call-box, phone for help.

Dinner – beef Stroganoff. I ate some of it to keep my strength up and poured some of the tea on to the carpet behind the bed.

I asked if I could have a bath and she graciously assented. Once inside, I noisily brushed my teeth, then, with a glance at the bathroom door, I knelt in front of the grill.

It *was* designed to open, I could see the hinges and a filled-in hole where the knob had been, and it had been filled-in some time before, so maybe Dr Kent was unaware of it. Air blew softly in my face. Should I try to open it now? I looked nervously round at the bathroom door again – probably better if I had the bath first.

I bathed quickly, dried myself and pulled nightie and dress-ing gown on, then knelt in front of the grill again and felt for the best hold. Gave a tug – nothing.

I turned on the tap for covering noise and tried again, harder. Still nothing. I turned the tap off and carefully examined the crack round the edge. A wooden wedge had been driven in to hold it, but a push from inside would probably free it, wouldn't it?

I needed more noise, so I leant over and operated the loo flush, then gripped the grill and heaved.

It flew open and I fell backwards, hitting the floor with my elbows. I pushed it shut with my foot . . . just in time. The bathroom door opened and Dr Kent came in.

"Are you all right, Miss Farewell?"

What about the wedge?

"I'm sorry," I said, "I slipped." I turned over, felt it under my knee, quickly palmed it and pushed myself up. "I got up from the loo and felt dizzy." I slid it into my dressing-gown pocket.

"Let me help you." She put a hand under my arm. "Had you just got out of the bath?"

"I – yes, before I used the loo."

"That explains it, then. Do you still feel dizzy?"

"A little . . . if I could just lie on my bed."

"Of course." She put a hand under my shoulder. "Are you hurt?"

"I'll probably have some bruises, otherwise I'm OK."

She helped me out past the silent Cal and back to my room. As soon as I'd taken off the dressing gown and she'd replaced the cuff, she said, "I'd better check you over."

"Really, there's no need."

"I insist."

I submitted while she eased my nightdress up. She ran her fingers skilfully over my elbows, shoulders and down my back. Her touch made me feel physically sick. I thought, I can't bear this, I'm going tonight.

"Everything's fine," she said. She poured a mug of water while I pulled my nightdress back down, then held out both the mug and her other hand. "Take these. I want you to get a good night's sleep." In her palm lay two sleeping tablets.

The irony, homunculus observed drily, *is that she's doing it as a precaution against you topping yourself, not because she suspects anything.*

I took them from her and placed them on the cabinet. "I'll take them in a minute."

"No, take them now."

"I wanted to read for a bit."

"Plenty of time for that tomorrow."

She means it. If you refuse, she'll get Cal and inject you with something.

"All right." Trying to keep the bitterness from my face, I sat on the bed, put a tablet in my mouth, raised the mug and swallowed. Repeated it with the second.

"Open your mouth," she said. She peered inside. "Lift up

your tongue . . . good. Now into bed with you and get a good night's sleep."

She turned down the light and locked the door behind her.

In my time as a nurse, I've seen every device there is used by patients who don't want to take tablets. The most effective is to tuck them behind your upper lip above your teeth and that was the method I'd used. I spat them into my hand, then eased out of bed to rinse my mouth into the chamber pot.

How long would they have taken to work? Half an hour? Better give it an hour.

I turned up the light, found *Tess* and took it back to bed with me, stared blankly at a page and thought, what shall I do first, the wire or the grill?

The wire – that way, if you can't get through it tonight, she won't realise.

God! The thought of another day here. I *must* get through it tonight.

Judging time was even more difficult than usual, but when I thought half an hour had gone, I let the book fall and lay my head on the pillow as though I'd fallen asleep reading it.

Would my slippers hold out? They were sheepskin, so they ought to. Should I look for something downstairs to wear on my feet? More clothes, even?

Time dragged, or did it? My face itched, I scratched it cautiously. Then my back itched as well . . . I tried to resist, but it got so bad I had to. Do we scratch in our sleep? I wondered. I was wasting time, she wasn't coming – why not get on with—

There was the slightest creak outside, then the lock clicked and the door opened. I tried to regulate my breathing. My heart was going so hard I thought she'd see the pulse in my neck. She approached and stood silently over me. I had to move, do something . . . I stirred, allowed the tiniest groan to escape my lips.

I felt her hands remove the book, pull up the duvet and tuck it gently round my shoulders.

Tom would have been proud of me.

Twenty-Six

The plastic coating was even tougher than I'd thought and before long my fingers ached so much I had to stop. My plan was to cut it all the way round in two places, then remove a cylinder of plastic to expose the wire. I started again, worked steadily and, after another rest, was rewarded by the scrape of file against metal. My fingers felt as though they were about to drop off and all I had left to do was to cut the plastic all the way round, repeat, remove the cylinder, file through the wires and find my way out.

Go on with you, jeered homunculus.

I kept working. Changed position to ease the cramp in my legs, resulting in the most excruciating pins and needles I'd ever had.

At last, one circle was complete. I started the next, about half an inch from the first.

My fingers seemed to have got stronger. I kept going and lost all sense of time. My mind began to wander and I found myself thinking about Tom, wondering whether he was looking for—

The point of the file dug painfully into the skin beside my nail.

That'll teach you to pay attention.

I rocked to and fro with my eyes shut, holding my finger, squeezing it, sucking the blood away.

Then I started again.

Time – how much did I have? I must have started before midnight, maybe even before ten. An hour had passed, maybe two. What about Dr Kent, would she look in during the night?

No. She thinks you took the tablets.

Second circle complete. I tried to force the point under the plastic to tear it, but only succeeded in stabbing myself again, this time in the palm. I had to cut it through longways. I changed position, bent the wire over my finger and started again.

I stopped to give my fingers a rest, drank some water, picked up the wire again and some time later had cut through enough to prise the cylinder away.

I closed my eyes and rested my hands in my lap a moment, then got up and used the chamber pot.

Just think, Jo, this could be the last time you have to do this.

Yeah. Back to the wire – insert file point under a single strand, twist and saw.

The first few were quite easy, but then it got progressively more difficult. Whether the file had become blunted or the purchase not so good I didn't know. The ends of severed wire kept stabbing the tips of my fingers until my hands were quite bloody. The last few wouldn't go at all. In frustration, I tried bending them to and fro, but they wouldn't break and I began snivelling.

Come on, Jo, what's a little discomfort—

A little . . . !

—a little discomfort compared with Kent's version of mummies and daddies?

Back to the wire. One by one the strands reluctantly parted, then the last two suddenly went together.

This is it, Jo.

I drank some more water and began pulling the bed out. The wheels squeaked alarmingly and I stopped. Bloody hell, was it going to do that every time? Pretty well, yes. I moved it inch by inch, listening intently between pulls, it depended really on whether either of them were directly below me. Nothing for it but to go on inching, stopping nervously between each one.

When the bed was far enough out, I got down and felt for the grill. The carpet was damp where I'd poured away the tea.

I pushed the point of the file through the wallpaper and pulled it downwards – it refused to cut, ripping noisily on either side of the file instead. Was it that noisy, or did all noise seem loud to me?

I tried laying the file against the paper and slitting through it. It seemed to work better, and as it fell away, air blew softly into my face from the grill. but would it open?

I gripped the slats and pulled. Not another wedge, *please*. No, with a slight crack, it swung open to reveal a space with rafters.

I stood up and looked round the room. There was nothing I needed. Drank more water. Used the pot again – so much for homunculus' prediction. I wrapped the wire round my wrist, tying it crudely before pulling the dressing-gown sleeve over it.

This is it, Jo . . .

For some reason, I suddenly felt the strangest reluctance to leave the room, was it fear of the unknown?

Can't be any worse than the known, can it?

I turned the light up as far as it would go then eased myself through the wall. I turned left, gave my eyes time to adjust, then began crawling along the rafters. They were about a foot apart and almost immediately, my dressing gown caught under my knees. I undid it, letting it hang on either side of me, but the same thing happened with my nightie.

That's the advantage of pyjamas.

Thanks. I backed through the wall and into the room again. I unwrapped the wire, passed it down through my sleeve and used it as a crude belt to hold nightie and dressing gown up. Then, through the wall again, a moment for eyes, and off.

The rafters dug into my bare knees and a splinter pushed its way into the ball of my thumb. I pulled it out with my teeth and went on crawling. Cool air from the eaves flowed over my skin – no wonder I'd been able to hear the blackbird. The light from my room got fainter as I approached the corner.

There was no obstruction, thank God, but the space after it was smaller, quite a bit smaller. I started to work my way round.

It was no longer possible to crawl, I had to worm and what little light there was faded altogether.

Potholing had never appealed to me much but this put me off forever. I had very little movement with each limb and the rafters soon dislodged my nightie and dressing gown from where I'd tied them, restricting me further, then my elbow slipped, knocking heavily against the plaster ceiling. I stopped and held my breath.

I suddenly realised that I couldn't go back even if I wanted to. I lost control and drew in a breath to scream.

Stop it, Jo. Think. You've got plenty of time. Just move six inches at a go and rest. You've got what? Another ten feet? Kid's stuff.

Kid's stuff. Splinters, abrasions on elbows and knees, filthy cobwebs and dust in my eyes, nose and throat. Total darkness. One of my slippers lived up to its name and slipped from my foot, but my toe was still touching it. I eased back an inch and wriggled my foot down into it.

Six inches at a time.

Six inches . . .

Time . . .

Then I perceived the tiniest glimmer ahead.

The bathroom door's open and there's a light on somewhere.

My first bit of luck.

I wriggled up to it. It was just as well I'd risked opening the grill earlier because I'd never have done it from where I was not without a making a lot of noise, anyway. As it was, it opened with barely a click and I curled my way into the bathroom where I just lay on the floor, letting every muscle go.

Come on, Jo, you haven't got all day.

Night, actually. I pushed myself to my feet. I was dry, desperate for a drink, but I didn't dare. Thank God I'd had some water earlier. I edged to the open door and through it. Light filtered up from below, the stairs beckoned – what the hell was that noise?

Snoring. One of them was snoring and had their bedroom door open. Cal.

Bloody *hell!*

I started down the stairs, keeping to the edge to avoid creaks (thanks, Tom) and turned ninety degrees on to a small landing. At the bottom was a wide passage, running the length of the bungalow. At one end was the front door – past Cal's room – at the other, a pool of darkness. Probably the kitchen. Which way should I go? Past Cal to the front door (known), or avoid Cal and go for the unknown?

The devil you know.

I crossed to the other side of the passage and a board let out a shriek. I forced myself to lift my foot very slowly and pressed myself against the wall. The snoring continued unchanged. I swallowed, closed my eyes and tried to calm my heart, then began stealing along the wall, a foot at a time. No noise, reached Cal's room – stopped.

It was ridiculous, he was no more likely to hear me as I passed his door than at any other time, and yet crossing that blank space required every milligram of nerve I could summon.

There. I kept going to the door. A cinch. Slipped the yale catch and eased it—

There was a bloody chain, I hadn't noticed it. I twisted the latch and shut the door again.

The snoring went on. I took the end of the chain, slid it along the groove and out. Slipped the latch again and opened the door.

Moonlight and air, lovely fresh air in my face. I was halfway out when I realised there was another problem. If I pulled the door to, the snap of the latch would probably wake him; if I left it unlatched, the door would swing open and the cold air would definitely wake him. I clenched my teeth and slid back inside. So near – oh, dear Lord, what am I going to do?

A wedge, you need a wedge.

Where the hell am I going to find a wedge?

In your pocket from the bathroom grill.

I found it, then turned the latch and brought the knob down to hold it. I slipped out again, held the wedge against the side of the door and pulled it to . . . and it held.

I heaved in a lungful of beautiful night air and looked round. The Range Rover stood to one side.

Don't even think about it, Jo.

Along a concrete path leading to a gate, it swung open and I stepped on to a track. I looked either way – up or down? Lights twinkled in the distance, but near enough for me – down.

I walked quickly. The track was rough but such was the headiness of freedom that I didn't care. Trees on a low bank rustled. A half moon rode high in the cloudless sky and stars twinkled in the horizon.

I stopped to rewind the wire round my wrist, there was a grunt from the other side of the bank and I jumped as a shape, a sheep, ambled away.

I glanced back, the bungalow was out of sight now, nothing but the sky and the inky black trees.

A tawny owl hooted, its long quavering call filling the night. My toe hit a stone and I doubled up in agony, clenching my teeth with the pain. After that, I walked more carefully in the middle where the weeds grew, their sharp, tangy scent reaching me as I crushed them. My slippers became wet with dew, which I didn't mind because my arches had begun to ache. Then the cool night air found its way through my night clothes. I shivered, stopped and wrapped the dressing gown more tightly round me.

A wood loomed and dark conifers closed in – silent, spooky, but no worse than what Dr Kent had in mind for me.

How far had I come? A mile? Shouldn't I have found a road by now? I seemed to be going deeper into the hinterland. I hesitated, but the trees thinned ahead so I kept going. The gradient steepened, then the wood ended abruptly and I found myself staring down at the silvery surface of a lake. It was perhaps half a mile ahead, half a mile wide and at least two miles long I couldn't see where it ended. There were no lights on this side and the scattering that twinkled on the other was no nearer than before.

All of which meant I had to turn back.

I wanted to sit down and cry, but homunculus, my mentor and tormentor had other ideas.

Just turn round, and go back. One foot in front of the other. You've been out less than an hour – you've got plenty of time.

I hear and obey, all wise . . .

The gradient, which had seemed quite gentle on the way down now pulled at my calves and thighs and my feet began aching in earnest.

Just take it slowly, Jo.

Not through this bloody wood I'm not!

It seemed to go on for ever; the shapes more menacing, the silence more sinister and I remembered Mole going into the wild wood in *The Wind in the Willows* and tried to smile.

At last I emerged. My arches ached abominably and after a few paces I stopped to—

Something brushed my face and I let out a tiny shriek. It was a bat, I could see them flitting about like the insects they were hunting. I took several deep breaths, swallowed, and started walking again, more slowly.

Bats fluttered. The owl called again, quite near. The small of my back began to ache as well, but at least I wasn't cold any more. I settled into a rhythm that the aches found bearable.

Left right, left right, past the rustling trees . . . The roof of the bungalow poked its way into the sky and I found myself slowing down. There were no lights, no noise.

Why should there be?

I glanced nervously at it and crouched as I passed the gate. My toe hit a stone that rattled away – I froze. Why did it have to happen *now*?

No sound from the bungalow . . . I stole away.

Telegraph poles.

They should have told you which way to go earlier.

Oh shut up! How much time had I wasted? An hour? More? Five minutes later, I found the road.

It was only a minor road but it *was* a road and where there's a road, there's houses, or so I told myself. Left or right? No lights. Try going up this time. Right.

One foot in front of the other, left right, left right.

The road levelled and banks rose on either side of me – bad news, in that I could neither see where I was going, nor hide if I heard a car coming.

Left right, left right . . . wonder what the time is? Wonder when they get up?

Now that I was walking on the level, my legs and back had stopped aching, but the arches of my feet were worse. I stopped, leant against the bank and massaged them, than went on. They still hurt.

The banks fell away and I could see across fields full of crops. I so wanted to rest my feet but my body had cooled and I knew I'd shiver and find it hard to get going again. A gateway – I had to sit down. I sat beneath it, leant against it, massaging my feet again. I rewound the wire on to my wrist where it had come away, and shivered. The owl called again, or was it a different owl? The shivering got worse – my bottom was wet where I was sitting. I forced myself up, climbed on to the gate and looked around.

Nothing. No lights, no buildings, just field after field and hills in the distance. I forced myself to start walking again.

Left right, left right . . . I lost all sense of time. I became oblivious to everything except the arches of my feet. Then the stars began to fade and I thought my senses were going until, with a shock, I realised it was dawn.

Dawn. Light rose quickly and with it the dawn chorus – birdsong so loud it was painful. My left slipper was coming apart. I stopped to look – the stitching had come away between sole and upper and my toes were sticking out. It had to happen, amazing they'd held out so long, really. Through the birdsong

The Gift

I became aware of another sound, a sort of rhythmic thumping . . . an engine?

I hobbled along, favouring the left foot as much as possible till I found another gate and clambered up it.

Just down there, a silo, an old barn, sheds – a farm! There had to be a road or track to it. I continued up the road as fast as I could – there – a signpost.

I forgot the slipper and broke into a run and the sole stripped away some more but it wasn't too bad on the tarmac.

The sign read Bryn Fferm and pointed down a tarmac drive. I could see the silo and the barn and started towards them, but there were stones and I couldn't hurry. The thumping got louder – some sort of stationary engine. I reached a gate, also bearing the legend Bryn Fferm. Ahead was a yard, at the other end, the barn with the silo attached to it, to the right was a cottage and to the left, a long, low shed that ran up to the barn. An ammoniacal smell filled the air. Beside the shed door was a red pickup and a man unloading it. He wore overalls and was old and grizzled. He stopped working as I approached, as well he might – dawn apparitions in fleecy dressing gowns were probably outside his experience.

"*Bore da*," he said, eyeing me warily, and my heart sank.

"May I use your telephone, please?" I said slowly, clearly and loudly, to make myself heard over the engine.

"*Pwy ydych chi? O ble ydych chi'n dod?*"

"Tele-phone." I took a pace towards him and made a dialling motion with my finger. He took a nervous pace back.

"*Teliffon?*" he said. "*Paham? Mae 'n ddrwg gen I. Mid wyf yn siarad Saesneg.*"

"Please," I begged, pointing at the cottage, "Telephone."

He began speaking again, then his eyes flicked away over my shoulder. I spun round as the Range Rover sped through the gate and bore down on us.

Twenty-Seven

One moment I was frozen to the ground, the next, I was running lead footed to the door of the long shed. I slammed it, heard a yale snapping shut and ran.

An overwhelming stench of ammonia; a partitioned pathway stretching ahead like a tunnel; chickens squawking wildly in their pens, feathers; the door smashing in behind me; a dead end. Another door on my right – I scuttled through, slammed it, found a bolt and rammed it across. It shuddered as Cal crashed into it. I looked round, frantically.

A tractor, a harvester, a loft directly above me and beyond it, a cathedral-like space – the old barn.

I ran between the harvester and the tractor. Cal smashed into the door again, but it held. I made for the huge double doors at the back and pulled at the wicket set into them. It was sealed up.

I stood there, paralysed.

The other wicket. See what they're doing.

I ran over to the main doors, cracked open the wicket and peered through.

Dr Kent was trying to talk to the farmer. Cal appeared from the chicken shed and pointed up to the barn. The farmer stared at him, shook his head and started walking toward the cottage. Cal came up behind him, chopped at his neck and he fell to the ground. Dr Kent pointed over to the cottage and Cal ran over to it.

I shut the wicket, sprang the yale and turned to look for another way out. I couldn't see anything and had to wait for my eyes to adjust. At the far end of the barn. I made out a ladder running up to a small platform with a door . . . the grain silo.

I ran over to it, up the iron ladder on to the platform. I'd lost a slipper and my foot hurt. I tried the door, but it was locked.

What now?

Too exposed up here.

Down the ladder again – the dressing gown got tangled in my legs and I jumped the last bit, hurting my bare foot. I hobbled across the barn, wondered whether to try and double back through the chicken shed, but as I reached the main doors, the wicket rattled. I panicked completely. A wooden ladder led up to the loft and I shot up it without thinking. The wicket shuddered as Cat tried to break it down, but it held.

The loft was piled with junk, ancient farm equipment.

You should have gone through the chicken shed – too late now.

Pencil beams of sunlight from the roof lasered through the dusty air. There was silence from below.

What was he doing? Was it possible to see out?

I looked round, but there were no holes or cracks in the tightly fitting boards of the walls.

He's gone to get the keys from the farmer.

And he could be back any second. There was no way out, nowhere left to go. One thing's certain, I thought, I'm not going back *there*. I'm not . . .

I tried to find a weapon. There was a click from below and I heard the wicket open.

I shrank down. Cal closed it gently and moved to one side, toward me, as he waited for his eyes to adjust.

He's almost directly below you – isn't there something you could drop on him?

Even if I could find anything, he was bound to hear me moving it. Suddenly, I saw beside me a broad, rusty blade, about four feet long by nearly a foot wide, with a hilt and wooden handles at one end (I found out later it was an old

211

hayknife). I touched the curved cutting edge. It was still sharp, the end pointed.

I raised my head. Cal was looking round now, concentrating on one area at a time. His eyes fastened on the wooden ladder beside him.

You realise the wire's come undone again and it's hanging down there?

I could see it going over the edge of the loft.

"Well, well, well lookey here." Cal boomed. "Are you comin' down, honey, or am I comin' up?"

Don't say anything, wait till he gets on to the ladder.

Cal chuckled. "Thinkin' 'bout it. I don' need to come up." The wire jerked at my wrist.

"All right, I'm coming." I said.

I pushed myself to my knees, gripped the handle of the hayknife and tried to ease it free from the other rusty metal. With a scraping noise, it moved.

"Come on, come on." He tugged at the wire again.

"I'm stuck."

"Guess I'll have to come and get you after all." The wire slackened as he stepped on to the ladder . . .

I heaved at the hayknife again, another scrape, then it was free. It was heavy. I gripped it round the metal hilt and crawled on my knees to the ladder.

"Calvin, are you all right?" Dr Kent's voice came from outside.

"I'm fine, I've found her."

I reached the ladder. He looked up at me and with both hands, I flung the hayknife at him like a spear. He twisted to one side, grunting as it flew past his head, the wooden handle struck his jaw, then hit the floor.

His hand flew up to his neck. I was sure I'd missed, that just the handle had caught him, then I saw the blood spurting between his fingers.

"Calvin?" Dr Kent's voice came again. "*Calvin . . .*"

He looked up at me again, a puzzled frown on his face. With

a bubbling cry, he fell, crashing on top of the hayknife, the gun flying from his hand.

I was on to the ladder in a flash, but before I could get to the bottom, there was a creaking groan as one of the main doors opened and I was blinded by the light streaming in.

With an anguished cry, Dr Kent knelt beside him. She touched the wound in his neck and felt feverishly for his pulse. She cradled his hand to her cheek, touching his face and I understood.

Go for the gun, urged homunculus, *jump . . .*

As though by telepathy, she snatched it up, pointing it at me. I remained on the ladder, still as death. As still as Cal . . .

She stood up and took a step towards me. The bones of her face stood out so that she became a facsimile of the *Walking Madonna.*

"You have killed my son," she said slowly, intensely, her lips moving but not her teeth. "From now on, without question, you will do exactly as I tell you, or I will kill you. This pregnancy, and further pregnancies, will proceed until you bear me another child. Do you understand?"

Say yes.

"Yes."

The air round us suddenly filled with insects. There was a *boom* and, with an expression of astonishment on her face, she crumpled on to the floor beside Cal.

Something stung my face.

I looked round. The farmer walked slowly towards me, holding a shotgun.

"*Ydych chi'n jawn?*" His expression showed he was asking if I was all right. I nodded. "Doctor," he said, "Polis." Then, pointing at himself, "*Cymreig.* Welsh."

As we walked slowly over to the cottage, I felt my insides knotting, as though I was starting a period.

Twenty-Eight

We were on the Isle of Anglesey.

The farmer released his wife, whom Cal had tied to a chair (and who could speak English), then phoned the emergency services and found me some clothes. I was shaking over a cup of hot, sweet tea when the sirens arrived. The police were first by a whisker; one of them had just time to say, "Ah yes, I think we've heard about you," before I was whisked away by the ambulance.

"I don't want a bloody sedative," I snarled at the paramedic. "OK?"

I got one just the same and didn't really come to my senses again until they'd extracted the lead shot from my face.

"Marcus . . . Tom!" I spoke with some difficulty through the dressings on my face. "How did you get here so quickly?"

I was in a room at the hospital, being kept in for observation.

"We flew," said Tom. "How are you, Jo?"

"The better for seeing you." I couldn't remember when I was last so pleased to see anyone. "How about you?"

"Fine, thanks. Mind if we sit down?"

"Please."

"What a mess," Marcus said. "I'm so sorry, Jo, I never imagined it could end like this." He studied my face. "Are you in much pain?"

"A sort of generalised faceache. Nothing I'm not used to."

They smiled and Tom said. "That's not true and you know it."

Marcus's expression became businesslike. "Can you tell us briefly what happened? Don't, if it hurts you to speak."

"It's all right." They listened carefully while I explained. Marcus shook his head and said again how sorry he was, then told me what they knew themselves so far.

"Carla, Chrystal and Nurse Lavington are in America, although we've no idea where. After you two were caught at Imber, they drove to the Channel Tunnel, where they left Tom unconcious in their van, then they caught a train to Gatwick . . ."

"Wait a minute," I protested, "you're going too fast." I turned to Tom. "How did they catch you?"

He smiled without humour. "They'd seen the car and guessed we'd try for the phone. They were waiting for me. They bopped me on the head, then doped me. The next thing I remember is waking up in the van in the station car park."

"That's why we thought at first that you were on the Continent," said Marcus.

"Whereas in fact, they'd caught a train going the other way, to Gatwick," said Tom.

"And all the time, Dr Kent had me in the bungalow," I said. "Was it hers? The bungalow."

"No," replied Marcus. "It belongs to a women's group she set up in Manchester. After they'd caught you and Tom, they knew they couldn't stay at the manor any longer. We think that Carla and the others just wanted to get away to the States – they'd been planning to transfer their operations back there anyway when the lease on the manor ran out, but that Dr Kent refused to let you go. So she decided to hold you in Anglesey until the others could make arrangements to get you over to America."

"How could they have possibly done that? They must have known I'd never go willingly."

"From what you've told us, I think that Dr Kent was hoping to persuade you."

I gave a snort. He smiled.

"I know, but I get the strong impression that by this time, she'd . . . well, gone completely off her trolley. Lost all contact with reality. Not really a laughing matter."

"No," I agreed, remembering our conversations at the bungalow. I shivered.

"Do you know yet who killed Mrs Murrell?" I asked.

Tom answered. "We're still piecing together the Catcott scenario, but we think that the lab technician, Chrystal, had a culture of the streptococcus, and that it was administered by Nurse Jenni Lavington."

Nurse Jenni . . .

"Will they catch them?"

"I don't know. If they do, there'll be the problem of extradition."

"God, I hope they do." I looked up. "Would you have found me if I hadn't escaped?"

"We'd have found the bungalow, certainly. The question is, would you have still been there?"

I stared at him. "You really think she could have got me to America?"

He glanced at Marcus, then said, "She could have got you over to the Irish Republic from here without too much trouble. After that, who knows?"

I shivered again.

I stared into the mirror. I looked as though I had a minor case of smallpox, although the doctors had told me that equally minor plastic surgery would soon put that right.

Davina Kent had, as she'd told me, been an only child and her mother had died when she was ten. Her father, the local squire had not re-married and she had continued living with him at Catcott.

At school, she had been a clever, although withdrawn child, rather plain and not particularly popular with the other children. This pattern had continued into her teens, then in 1959, aged fourteen, she had been taken away from school for several months with the explanation that she was going on a trip.

She had left Catcott at the age of seventeen to study medicine at Liverpool and had not returned until after her father's death. Enquiries revealed that although her medical work had been brilliant and her energies prodigious, her hostility towards men had made it virtually impossible for them to work with her. The story she had told me was essentially true, but her bias had made some of her medical decisions questionable, to say the very least.

Calvin Moore had apparently been adopted by an American couple in 1960, although they couldn't produce adoption papers. DNA testing proved not only that Cal had been Dr Kent's son, but that her father had also been his. She had traced him while on sabbatical in America.

At times, I felt an overwhelming pity for her. At other times, when the things she had done to me were burning holes in my brain, I could feel nothing but loathing. The fact that I had actually killed someone bothered me at first, but then I realised that what I'd done was no different from the reaction of a person drowning – you just grab at anything that will save your life.

Professor Fulbourn had examined me minutely on my return and told me I was no longer pregnant. In fact, the tests could not conclusively show that I ever had been. As time goes by, I become more convinced that I never was. Wishful thinking, perhaps. As the Prof says, it's not the kind of technology he would wish to try and duplicate. What bothered me was that somewhere, Carla and Chrystal and Nurse Jenni were probably itching to do just that.

None of them had been traced. It seemed ironic that Cal, who'd never actually killed anyone was killed himself, but Nurse Jenni, a cold murderess, if ever there was one, was still free.

The other two nurses were found, but in the end, no charges were brought against them. They claimed ignorance, and because they'd stayed in Britain when the others had fled, nothing could be proved against them. Brian, the other security guard, was also found and arrested. He, too, claimed ignorance and so far, had only been charged with assault. The anaesthetist, Dr Longstreet, and Leila seemed to have been genuinely innocent – Tom had been right about her.

The only good thing to come out of it all was Denny and Geoff. After what Denny had been through, Geoff agreed to donor insemination, but before this could take place, she discovered that she was pregnant anyway, by Geoff.